BEAT AND LEON THE WARRIOR DOG

Into the Sassanid Empire and Beyond

Cy Sansum

authorHOUSE®

AuthorHouse™ UK
1663 Liberty Drive
Bloomington, IN 47403 USA
www.authorhouse.co.uk
Phone: UK TFN: 0800 0148641 (Toll Free inside the UK)
UK Local: (02) 0369 56322 (+44 20 3695 6322 from outside the UK)

Published by AuthorHouse 05/23/2022

ISBN: 978-1-6655-9888-0 (sc)
ISBN: 978-1-6655-9887-3 (e)

Print information available on the last page.

CONTENTS

ACKNOWLEDGEMENT

I continue to be supported by these amazing ladies. Without them, The Leon books would not exist.

Jennifer Dominise: Account specialist/senior publishing consultant.
Jennifer continues to provide me, with encouragement.
Throughout the book, she continues to give support.
She is always there to answer my questions.

Katie Hoolahan: Editor.
This talented lady skilfully edited this book, as she did with the previous Leon book.
She has amazing abilities, which bring my books to life.

INTRODUCTION

My Name is Beat.
I used to live high up in the Swiss alps, where I looked after my father's sheep.

There were often attacks by Wolves, especially during the winter months.

My father has a pack of Anatolian Shepherd dogs.

The leader of the pack was Leon. Leon was the youngest but also strongest, cleverest, and my best friend.

If you read the previous book (Leon the warrior dog). Leon and I, had to join the Roman Army. We participated in many adventures, and many battles. At one point, I was leading a small group of Roman soldiers, in a back to the wall defence of Rome itself.

Our Emperor Constantine, had declared that the religion of the Roman Empire, was now Christian. Therefore, all citizens had to become Christians. Can he really order us to become a Christian? Surly a man's religion is what is in their heart.

Rome was about to fall. All the people had done their best, but the Goths, outnumbered us and Rome was about to be destroyed.

I had made one of my first prayers to this Christian God. Lia had often spoke about this Jesus, now I have no other option, but to trust him.

About a half hour after, I made my prayer. To my surprise and excitement, I could hear the sound of many war cries!

Charging towards the back of the Goth army, were Thousands of Alemanni warriors, led by the love of my life, Princess Sky.

Sky, had managed to persuade her father, to let her take Warriors, to fight against the Goths.

After the Saving of Rome. Sky, myself, and of course Leon, returned to visit my father, before travelling north to Sky's Home. There we were soon married.

Every day was peaceful, lying beside a stream, or running through a Sunkissed meadow.

Then the bad news!

On day the emperor made a visit, and asked, or rather ordered me to take charge of the Eastern Roman Army. He wanted me to lead the Eastern army, against the Sassanid Empire.

The Sassanid empire, was the last pre-Islamic Persian Empire. The Sassanid Empire extended from Modern day Turkey to modern day Pakistan. Their soldiers, had crossed into the Eastern Roman Empire and taken Jerusalem. My orders were, to drive them out of Jerusalem. And then to Destroy the Sassanid Empire.

My target, was to enter the Sassanid Capital, and then capture, or kill, their Emperor. Now that is easy to talk about but to deliver would be a massive challenge.

while I was thinking about this order, Lia came into the room. If you had read the previous book, you will be aware that Lia, and her sister Tia, where daughters of a Senator. They had both been captured by a breakaway group of rebel Alemanni warriors. Both of the young women were going to be sacrificed to the Alemanni Gods.

Eventually, I was told that one would be burnt to death, while the other would be freed. I was given the job of asking Tia, to reject this Jesus, then she would be saved from the stake, and set free. (What she did not know, was that if she rejected Jesus, her sister Lia, would be burnt in her place). Tia, refused to reject Jesus and was burnt.

I will never forget the look on her face. There were no tears or screaming. It was as if someone was shielding her from the pain. she just stood there, as the flames enveloped her.

I still see her face, every night in my dreams.

The emperor ordered me, to take Lia with us, to Jerusalem. Lea, was eventually given the role of making sure, all my soldiers were Christians.

After a couple of battles, we arrived at Jerusalem.

It had taken a bit of cunning, and pain, to break into the city.

Now we are preparing for the Invasion of the Sassanid Empire.

CHAPTER ONE

INTO THE SASSANID EMPIRE

I t was early morning. I was standing on top of a hill overlooking the road that the Eastern Roman army will use in its quest to conquer the Sassanid Empire. I was once Beat, the shepherd boy, but now I am Commander Zug of the Eastern Roman army, and planning the campaign for the invasion.

The year was 315AD, in early September. I had already achieved one part of our Emperor's command, which was to capture Jerusalem. That was in fact the easy part. Now, I was about to lead the Roman Eastern Army on a mission to teach the Sassanid Empire a lesson. My orders were to destroy their armies, and ensure that the Sassanid were unable to invade Roman territory, ever again. The Sassanid Empire covered a massive area.

I had started out from Antioch with 220,000 soldiers, plus another couple of thousand warriors from other tribes. Our losses had been few from the long march, but after leaving 50,000 soldiers behind to protect Jerusalem, my fighting force was reduced to about 155,000 soldiers.

I intended to avoid the direct route to their Capital, by marching south then crossing the Nafud desert. This would hopefully avoid any battles before we reached their capital.

My plan was to cross the Nafud Desert during late Autumn when it would be cooler and we may be able to find an Oasis, or two, with some water. My army was large, with many men and horses to provide for. This all has to be transported.

I would commandeer our supplies from the neighbourhood, but somehow, we would need to restock regularly, which could be a problem.

Water would be limited, food may also be in short supply, and we would be fighting a larger army, often protected by high walled cities. This would be a bit of a challenge.

I was joined by Leon.

"Hello boy," I said to him, "have you come to help me, or are you just getting a break from your missus?" I smiled. I even thought I saw a smile on Leon's face.

Ok, I know dogs don't smile, but it did look like a smile. Leon jumped onto me, and knocked me over. I grabbed him around his chest, and we rolled around for a bit.

"Leon my friend, we haven't had a wrestle for ages! Although you always win, it's nice to have a wrestle with you, it takes my problems away for a while."

I was now sitting with Leon lying next to me. He didn't give much advice, but I did feel more relaxed. It wasn't long before my thoughts returned to the concerns I had before Leon turned up. Being a shepherd boy protecting my sheep from the Wolves was a lot easier than being a Roman officer. I was now holding my head in my hands, looking a bit lost. Then I heard Sky calling me.

"You look like you need some help." she said.

I threw my arms around her and held her close.

"I am afraid I do." I replied. "We have an army of about 160,000 men, and about 200,000 horses. Somehow, we have to feed and water them. We will be crossing a land, where few Romans have been before, and none of my people, or your people have crossed. We don't know how many battles we will have to fight, and have no way of replacing any soldiers which we may lose."

"Yes, my love, you do have a bit of a problem." Sky replied.

"No problem though, you married a handsome and wise husband. And I have a plan."

"I have arranged for a meeting at noon, where I will disclose my plan. Until then let's enjoy this peaceful moment, there won't be many of those for the foreseeable future."

It was noon. The time I spent with Sky seemed to have flown by. I had invited Lia, Mae, and Sky of course, plus Marcus, Quintin, and two other generals, Julius and Anthony.

I started the meeting by reminding the gathering about what Alexander the great had done in the year 334 BC. When they crushed the Persian Empire and even advanced into India. I continued by allocating the task of collecting enough water and food for a 200-mile journey for both men and horses, to one of my younger generals. Then I explained my plan.

"We will march south, to our friends the Ghassanids. They are allies of Rome. Hopefully, we can restock our supplies there, and maybe acquire some men as scouts. Also, we will buy camels, and transfer the food, and water from the horses to the camels. Eventually, the army will march across the Nafud desert. Hopefully avoiding any major battles.

"At a given point, we will turn north and march to where there should be a small river, where we will again fill our water containers. After a rest we will continue until we reach the mighty Euphrates River. Here we will rest and make lots of Black Powder. This will come in use later.

"After making the black powder, we will march south following the Euphrates. Then at the point where the Euphrates meets the Tigris, we will march north to the Sassanid Capital city, Ctesiphon. With the help of the black powder, we will capture their capital, and take control of their Empire."

"That does sound very simple," said Sky.

"Yes, it does, but only on paper. The biggest problem will be crossing the Desert. 55°C during the day, and below freezing at night - not to mention the Desert winds. Also, maybe a few of the tribesmen will make attacks - although I doubt if they will make a frontal charge, more of a hit and run tactic. We must make sure we have enough water, until we come across an oasis, or get to the river which runs north towards the Euphrates."

"Any questions?" I asked.

"Yes." replied Mae. "We have only so much black powder left, I will need to make more if we are going to destroy their Empire".

"As I said earlier, you will be able to make a large supply of black powder, before the army arrives at the Euphrates. I have information that Potassium Nitrate and Sulphur can be found about ten miles from the Euphrates. Charcoal can be made anywhere."

Anthony then asked another question.

"Why, sir, are we going to travel through that desert? Surely it would be easier to travel directly to the Sassanid capital?"

"True Anthony," I replied. "But we would have them out in the open. Our enemy would also know our numbers, where we are, and they would then hold all the aces. By travelling across part of the Nafud Desert, we hopefully will be able to surprise our enemies when we re-appear beside the Euphrates."

"It is late summer now, so we will be crossing the desert in early winter, thus we won't be travelling during the heat of summer. Also, there may be a few oases where we can replenish our water supplies.

As there were only those two questions, I turned and spoke with Sky.

"Sky. I am going to make a visit to my friends the Ghassanids. Their leader, Frome, came to my father's house and asked if he could buy Leon. Leon wanted to stay with me, but we did become friends. I want to take 50 of your warriors with me. I hope that is ok"

"My love," she replied," you can take many more if you need. There will be enough Romans here to protect me"

"Fifty will be enough. I plan to leave at dusk and travel by night"

As the sun sunk behind the horizon, the moon started to appear. It seemed to light up the night sky. Fifty of Sky's best warriors were waiting for my order to leave, but I was still one short. However, it wasn't long before he came running over. Yes, Leon would not be left behind on this trip.

Although we all had horses, it would still be a long journey. I expected to meet up with King Frome in his Town by early afternoon. We were leaving at dusk, as I was hoping that anyone who may want to attack us would be asleep. I gave the order to trot! It would be a long journey there and back.

Riding at night can feel very eerie. Everywhere is black apart from the moonlight and strange sounds could be heard every now and then. I was glad when the sun rose again.

The Ghassanids were friends of Rome but most people in this area were not. It was just past noon when I noticed a head appearing from behind rock on a nearby hill. We were only a few hours short of arriving at our destination. I knew the warriors which Sky had sent were her best fighters and they would give their lives to protect me.

As we rode silently, through the night, I could feel many eyes piercing my back. At the end of the valley, I halted the group and ordered the men to take a rest for two hours. I knew there could be enemies everywhere, but I still decided to walk around the outside of our camp, where there was the stillness of the early morning. I needed to clear my mind.

The men were resting before starting on the last leg of our journey. The rays of the morning sun lit up our camp and my mind started to wander. That was my second mistake.

The first was to wander too far from camp, the second, which could have been my last, was to lose concentration. I was soon surrounded by six Arabs, they knocked me on the head with something very hard, to silence me.

I woke to find myself tied to a pole in the middle of a tent. I counted six burly guards with massive swords. A flap opened and in came the man who I presumed was their leader.

"You are a fool to wander about alone in the dark!" he said. "You will tell me *now* where you are going with such a small force"

"That, my friend, is for me to know and you to find out" I replied.

"Have no fear my friend, I intend to visit your men and inform them that I plan to cut you to pieces unless they surrender."

"Well, you had better kill me now! I told my men that if anyone, and that includes me, gets captured, they must be left to die".

"You are a brave man, Roman, but when your men see me start to peel your skin off your chest, they *will* surrender".

"I will see you in the morning. Have a nice sleep" he replied as he left the tent.

That was that, I was tied up, and my men would not be able to rescue me. Sky would kill me if she was here, for falling into this trap. There I was sitting on the ground, while watching the Guards. I started to lose faith in any rescue. I didn't have much time for this world. 'I will give Lia's God a call', I thought. He had answered my requests in the past.

As soon as I had finished my prayer, I heard a scratching noise. And then a head popped up from under the tent.

"Leon! My hero, you have come to save me".

The Guards did not stand for long, swords don't worry my Leon. He then quickly chewed through the ropes which held my hands together, and sat in front on Guard. I untied my feet and was free!

I told Leon to be quiet as we headed out in search of my warriors. Once we were all gathered, I ordered my warriors to be ready for battle (these warriors are always ready for battle). While I had been a guest of the enemy, my warriors had been checking their strength. It turns out they only had thirty men, to my fifty warriors. The advantage was now mine. I decided to set a trap.

The plan was to send twenty of my warriors along the path. Hopefully, they would think that this was my entire force. Then when they attack, the rest of my warriors would fall on them.

The plan worked well. As I and my twenty warriors rode slowly along the path, the Arab tribesmen made their attack.

My warriors had been waiting for this fight, they were all ready for action. They would not want to be part of any defensive formation.

I ordered my men to form a line. I had been remembering the threat to peel off my skin. I held my sword high and gave the order.

"CHARGE!"

My warriors smashed into the enemy, horses were neighing, swords slashing left and right and blood was everywhere.

Leon could not run as fast as the horses, but he arrived in time to join the fight before the last few Arabs surrendered.

I was very pleased that none of my warriors were killed, although they all had various cuts and bruises.

I know that Sky would not have been pleased if any more of her warriors did not return. While first aid was being administered, the rest of my men arrived. They were moaning, that we should have left a few for them to kill. I looked up from where I was sitting and having my arm treated.

"I'll tell you what. The next fight we get into, you can do all the fighting and we will watch and learn how great fighters you all are." I finished with a smile.

It was only about another hour until we arrived at the main town of the Ghassanids. The first man to meet us was their leader Frome. He looked the same man that I had met at my father's house, maybe five years ago.

Frome threw his arms around my chest, and almost crushed me with his hug.

Leon then joined us as he was wondering if I was being attacked.

"I see you still have that giant mutt," Frome said. "Are you going to sell him to me now?" he asked with a smile on his face.

"My friend, there isn't enough money in the world to buy him. But he is his own master. If you can get him to go with you, then I would have lost my best friend, and you would have gained one".

Frome replied that he could not take a man's best friend away from him, and after grabbing my arm, pulled me towards a table covered in food and wine.

It was the biggest table that I had ever seen, all of my warriors were seated. We talked about my mission and the plan I had put together. Then slapping my back, Frome told me that he would lend me 10,000 of his warriors. They were good fighters and they knew the Nafud desert. But he then made a request.

"My daughter must go with my warriors; she is a bit head strong but she is a great fighter and knows the Nafud desert well."

I shook Frome's hand, while thanking him for his help.

I had decided to leave at dawn the following day.

Frome had arranged a meal for us before we left, and said that he would introduce his daughter, Princess Deana.

I gave orders for the horses to be fed, and for my warriors to rest for the rest of the day. I personally found a mound of sand where I was able to take a rest.

As I was daydreaming, I saw a dark-haired woman wearing an Egyptian style dress walking towards me. Her figure was athletic, she reminded me of my Darling Sky. This woman walked up to where I was laying and held out her hand.

"I am Deana, I believe my father has told you about me. I will be joining you for your campaign against the Sassanid army".

I shook her hand. She had a good strong grasp.

"May I sit with you for a while"? she asked.

"My pleasure" I replied, "I get the impression that you are a lady that likes fighting".

"Yes, I do" was her reply, "and it's a nice change to fight alongside such a handsome General".

I started to feel a little hot. If Sky was here now, I think there would soon be a fight.

"Deana, we leave at dawn. Pick ten of your best scouts and send them into the Nafud desert. I need to know what is going on by the time my army reaches the desert".

"Yes, no problems. I will lead my fathers' warriors, under your leadership of course!" she replied.

I thanked her, then told her that I was going to have an early night. Now where is Leon? Looking for food I bet.

I had a room to myself; well Leon shared my room. That night I was lucky that he was with me. I was sleeping on a pile of sheets laid on the floor. Today it had been hot and sunny and I was still sweating, even though it was evening. I was only wearing my loincloth, as I tried to find a cool sheet to lay on.

I was finally starting to fall asleep when I felt something brush against my head. I started to raise my head when Leon landed on top of me.

It was clear what had happened. Leon was laying across my chest with part of a Cobra, in his mouth. If the snake had bit me, that would have been the end of my career. I would have died here far away from the mountains of home. As the snake was about to strike, good old Leon had leapt across my bed and bitten the snake just below its head.

Once again, I am indebted to Leon for saving my life. I threw my arms around him.

Then the door opened wide and there stood Deana.

"Looks like I have arrived just in time" she said.

"Why is that?" I replied. I looked down to see why Deana was laughing - my Loincloth had come apart as Leon jumped across me to get to the snake. Quickly I wrapped a large piece of a sheet around my waist.

My face was now bright red, I was so embarrassed.

"Don't be embarrassed" said Deana "I have seen a few men's bodies."

"Maybe. But not mine!" Then I had a horrible thought, Sky would kill me if she ever found out.

We were all ready to march just after the sun rose. Frome had given us many camels.

"They will be so helpful when you travel across the desert!" he said.

"My Friend Frome, you have given us so much, how can I ever thank you?" I told him.

"That's easy," Frome replied, "bring my daughter back safe."

"That I promise you. I will bring her home to you my friend" I pledged.

We made it back to Jerusalem as fast as we could. The first thing I did was to introduce Deana to Sky, Lia and Mae.

"So, you are Beat's wife" supposed Deana "Your husband had a lucky escape the other night."

I was now staring at Deana.

"Why what happened?" asked Sky.

"He was attacked by a large snake." Deana replied.

I was now turning red again and praying that Deana would not say anything more.

"Well," continued Deana, "it was a very hot day and your husband decided to wear very little clothing".

Then to my horror, Deana gathered the girls up close to her, and whispered something in their ears.

All four of them looked at me and started to laugh. It was Mae who spoke first.

"It was lucky that Leon was around to save you again."

Ah! Just about the snake. That's ok, I thought.

Then Sky asked a question.

"Will you use the snake skin to make any night clothes my love?"

They know, I thought. I quickly turned and rushed towards the door, muttering something like "I have to check that the sentries are set out ok".

As I left the room, all I could hear was women's laughter.

The cool night air was what I needed. I wandered around the camp and everything looked secure. Then I saw Anthony and Julius talking together. They were both discussing Mae.

These two generals had been away with the Army for over two years. Young beautiful women can be a distraction. I listened unknowingly to them.

They had both decided that Sky was unavailable, as she was my wife. Leaving Lia, Mae and Deana. Deana was the daughter of a friendly power, so best to avoid her. Leaving Lia and Mae. They both knew that Quintin and Marcus were wanting after Lia, so that left Mae.

At this point I interrupted them.

"Just to let you know lads, Mae is married with 3 children."

"But..." Replied Julius, "her husband is a very long way from here. And a lot of battles will be Fought before she returns. She may not get back to her husband."

I now moved close to face these two officers.

"Just to let you know my friends, Mae is possibly the most important part of this army. And I have promised her that I will get her back to her family. So, the both of you should have regular cold swims! Be warned."

Both men saluted, apologised and walked away.

Later I returned to my room where Sky was ready for bed.

"Don't worry my love, accidents do happen", she said lovingly.

I was lost for what to say.

"And," Sky started to speak again. "Deana said you have a great body".

I now most definitely did not know what to say, or do.

Then Sky spoke again.

"Would my husband like to share it with me?" At this point I knew exactly what to do. I was embarrassed no longer.

CHAPTER TWO

FAREWELL JERUSALEM

C amels are known as the ship of the desert. I totally understood the meaning of this as we were crossing the Nafud Desert.

The original plan was for the whole army to march north from the desert towards the river Euphrates. During our march we would stop and collect the necessary chemicals to make the black powder. However, Mae pointed out to me that it would be better if a small party looked for the chemicals, as that would draw less attention. It made sense, so I put together a small group to collect the ingredients for the black powder. But also, a group that I had confidence in.

Mae was the Scientist, but she was also good at martial arts, and Sky had taught her how to use a sword. She used to hunt animals for food when she lived with the old man. She was the obvious choice to put in charge of the task. Next, I chose Deana, a top fighter who also knew the country. From Rome, I added General Anthony, another skilled fighter who knew Roman tactics. Last was someone who was new to me. Sky recommended him; His name was Kuuli. Kuuli, had been Sky's personal bodyguard, before we were married.

"He is a brilliant fighter and has a nickname". She had said.

"What is that my love?" I asked.

"He is known as the silent assassin. And don't ask why." she replied.

"Ok, I won't". I don't think I wanted to know.

I also allocated what was left of Sky's personal guard, and a thousand Ghassanid warriors.

The plan was that we would all travel together, then at an arranged point, Mae's group would break away, leaving the slower moving bulk of the army to follow as fast as they could.

As we journeyed south towards Deana's town, El Shaffar, Deana rode up alongside my horse.

"Beat," she said, "would you like me to share some information about the Nafud desert."

"That would be very helpful," I replied.

"Well," began Deana, "the surrounding hills are made of iron oxide, which eventually formed the sands of the Nafud Desert - Mae, can tell you more about that. This is what gives it a unique reddish colour. This desert is also known for sudden violent winds, creating large crescent shaped dunes. Winter rain produces grasses sufficient to support grazing in winter and spring."

"Also," she continued, "the Nafud desert is about 180 miles long. If you plan to break away from the desert, just over half way across, you may have a hundred miles to travel."

"I plan to break away from the desert, by turning north about halfway across the desert, and heading to the river Euphrates" I told her "Therefore we will have a long walk. I am glad I am not a foot soldier."

Of course, leading a massive army across this desert would not be easy, even with a horse.

I started to remember the first time I rode a horse. Looking after my father's sheep high up in the mountains didn't require a horse.

The first time I had to ride a horse was a nightmare. Riding was easy enough, but my sore bottom. Now I have ridden so many miles, my bottom is like leather.

Eventually we arrived at Deana's town. I had arranged with King Frome for us to stay with him until late November. This, of course, would give my friend problems, as he would need to provide food, water, and shelter for my army.

King Frome soon showed what a true friend he was. He provided for all our needs, without any complaint. However, he told me about another problem that he did have.

As I have said before, the Ghassanids are friends of Rome. But their neighbours were not. In particular, King Frome was having problems with the Egyptians. There had been several raids by Egyptian soldiers.

"Frome, my friend, I think we will have to do something that will cripple their armies."

However, I had no desire to send my whole army against them, as I would need all my soldiers to crush the Sassanid army.

I called Deana and Marcus, to my quarters.

"Which is the most important target?" I asked Deana, "What would cause the most damage to the Egyptian army?"

Deana thought for a while, then banged her fist on the table.

"The Egyptians need their war chariots to attack my people. There is a large town about fifty miles from here where they make most of their war chariots. If we set fire to their workshops, that would be a massive setback for them and they wouldn't be able to attack my people for a very long time!"

"That's brilliant!" I replied. "How many men would we need for our fire raid?"

"It would require your light cavalry; they can move fast and they are good archers."

"Will two hundred, be enough?" I asked.

"Yes." Replied Deana.

"We will depart just as the sun is setting. We can travel at night and surprise them before they wake up."

"Both of you be ready. Marcus, please inform the light cavalry that I require two hundred riders, ready before sunset for a night excursion".

At that point the door flew open and Sky and Mae walked in. Sky came round behind me and put her arm around my shoulders. Her other arm, or rather hand, ran through my hair.

"My love" she said, "are you planning to let me sleep alone tonight?"

I was now getting a bit nervous; I was wondering what to say.

"We have to do some damage to the Egyptians, as they are causing the Ghassanids problems." I finally replied.

"That's ok my love," Sky replied. "I presume you are about to ask me and Mae to join you?"

"Well, I don't want you to get hurt, and Mae is important to make the black powder".

At this point, Sky kissed me on the cheek. That's it, I knew I had lost.

"Ok, you can both come with us. Get horses and be ready at sunset."

It's so unfair, women talk nice and kiss you, then they get whatever they want. I may as well have just asked them in the first place. I turned to Sky, and asked her if she had some time to spend with me.

"I would, my love, but I have to prepare for the journey now," and out the door she went.

I sometimes wonder if I am the Commander of this army, or if Sky, and the other Women, are really in charge.

Then I had an idea, I would add another man to this little trip, he may give me some support. I sent a message for Kuuli to come and see me.

He arrived in no time at all. I shook his hand and welcomed him. We had a long chat. It wasn't long before I realised that I liked this man. Curiosity got the better of me.

"Tell me Kuuli, why are you called the silent assassin?" He smiled, then replied "It's simple. I can kill anyone without being seen, or heard."

"I think you could be very useful tonight" I replied.

As he was about to leave, he turned to me with a big smile and held out his hand. "I was Princess Sky's bodyguard since she was a child," I want you to know that I am very pleased that she married you, because I know you love each other and you will always look after her."

"Thank you, my friend." I replied.

Later that afternoon, I went for a walk. As I approached the house where Deana and Mae were staying, I witnessed a conversation between Julius and Mae.

Mae was standing just outside her house, while Julius was standing a few feet away.

"While we are on this campaign, would you like us to be 'friends?" asked Julius.

"No thanks," replied Mae.

"It will be a long way. You may want some male company" suggested Julius.

"Julius, I have a husband who I love very much, and three children, who make my heart beat. My only wish in life is to return to them."

"That's ok," proclaimed Julius, "It will just be a close friendship until we return to Rome".

I was now looking at Mae's eyes, as she stared at Julius. Only once before in my life, had I seen eyes like those. It was about 4 years ago. I went with my father and Leon to North Africa, as my father wanted to buy some sheep". On arrival, my father met up with the owner of the Sheep. While they were doing business, Leon and I went for a walk. We found a hill with some ledges half way up. We both managed to get up to a ledge and lay there in the sun.

My curiosity was aroused with the arrival at the bottom of the hill, of a lioness with her three cubs. Both Leon, and I lay quietly watching what was about to unfold. A small path ran through the mountain. The lioness was trying to make her cubs run down the path as quickly as possible. At that point two large male lions arrived. They were probably brothers that had been kicked out of their pride. The Mother of the Cubs knew that the males would kill her cubs, so she chased them down this path, then positioned herself at the entrance, so as to prevent the males from following them. The path the Lioness chose was narrow, and difficult for more than one full grown male lion to pass. The Males decided to challenge her one at a time.

As the first male approached, that was when I saw the look in the eyes of the Lioness - the look of a mother who would give her life willingly, to save her children. This was what I saw in Mae's eyes that day.

The male Lion was very large but the lioness took him on. Somehow, she managed to kill the male, but she was hurt, and bleeding. At this point the second male came in for the kill.

I looked at Leon and winked. He knew what I was saying. We both slid down to the ground below. I fired an arrow which hit the lion in his side. I did not have time for a second shot. The lion was upon me.

I had a knife which I drove into its stomach. By then I was on my back, with the lion injured but still very much alive, I smelt his foul breath in my face.

This was one of the first times, of many, that Leon had saved my life.

Leon jumped onto the lion's back and bit it on the back of its neck. I could hear the crack of the neck breaking.

The lioness was on her way down the path to find her cubs. She looked ok, I thought. At that point, she looked back at us, as if to thank us, then re-joined her cubs. When a mother is defending her family, she will move heaven and earth to save them.

Suddenly, Mae moved forward, in a split second, and hit Julius straight in the nose! Blood was spurted everywhere. She had broken his nose.

"Keep away from me now, or next time I will break other parts of your body. Be warned!" At that, Mae slammed her door shut.

Julius staggered away holding his bleeding nose.

Knock, knock. Marcus banged on Lia's door until the door finally opened.

"Hello Marcus," said Lia.

"Would you like to go for a walk with me?" asked Marcus.

"Marcus, it's only fair to tell you that I have told Quintin to court me again. We were about to be married a few years ago. I have to give him a chance to prove that he still loves me - I still want to marry him. So, Marcus, although I think you are a nice man, I can't allow us to get close until I have given Quintin a final chance".

Marcus was feeling dejected, but managed to reply

"If that's what you want to do, then I will wait until you decide where your feelings lie".

"Take care Lia, if you need me, I will be here for you." Then he turned and walked away.

The sun had started to fall behind the clouds. It was time for us to ride into the night, and hopefully cause a bit of damage to the Egyptians.

We had about fifty miles to ride tonight. I believed this should take us two or three hours. My plan was simple: on arriving, maybe a mile from the town, Sky, Mae, Deana, Kuuli and I would head towards one of the fences. We would all slip over the fence and head towards the area, where the war Chariots were being made.

I had asked Mae to bring a few bags of her black powder along. I intended for Mae to explode them on my signal.

At the sound of the explosion, one hundred of my light cavalry, led by Marcus, would charge through the gate, and join us in burning the Chariots. The rest of my light cavalry would dismount, and prepare to support our retreat after we had burnt down the town.

The five of us crept towards a part of the fence which looked to be in an area not lit up by the moon. I said the five of us, but there were really seven of us. Leon and Beaue can't run as fast as a horse, so I had a cart prepared for them.

Once we had all cleared the fence, we gathered to discuss our next move. This was a town, but it was not a big town, as it was only used to make war chariots, and accommodate the workers. We could clearly see the building where the chariots were made, and there were hundreds of new war chariots parked around the building.

"My friend Kuuli, you will be the first to see action. I want you to go ahead and remove any guards. Let's see how silent my silent assassin is!" I laughed.

I gave him a twenty-minute head-start. Now it was time for the rest of us to get involved. At that point, Leon and Beaue arrived.

We had decided to start by burning the building where the war chariots are built. I sent Leon and Beaue ahead, to make sure we would have a clear way to the building. Fifteen minutes later, we were at the door of the building.

While Sky, and Deana, prepared to shoot fire arrows towards the chariots, I turned to Mae.

"Are you ready with your bombs?" I asked. Mae replied by holding out the three bags of black powder.

Mae put the three bags beside a chariot, then inserted a piece of what looked like string, she lit the string and ran. The black powder exploded with a massive Bang!

At that point, I could hear the pounding of soldiers, hurrying towards us. As all the chariots were now on fire, I thought it would be best to make our stand outside the building.

Sky and I were fighting back-to-back and Mae and Deana were doing the same a few feet away from us. Let's not forget Leon and Beaue, they were more than doing their bit. I was starting to worry as I had not yet seen Kuuli. Then he came into view, with a large smile on his face.

"All taken care of Sir." Kuuli beamed.

"Well done!" I told him. "And my name is Beat, to my friends."

I could not resist telling Sky, "I don't think he was that silent tonight; he was stabbed at least a couple of times".

There must have been forty or fifty Egyptian soldiers running towards us. The odds were against us, unless Marcus arrived soon.

The fighting soon became bloody, I had a cut across my right arm, and a sword slashed my side. Sky had a couple of cuts, but she also took an arrow in her back, just above her heart. Then, just in time, my cavalry came into view.

Marcus was in the lead with his sword slashing left and right. Ten riders stopped where we were making our stand. We all jumped up behind a rider, and all galloped off as soon as the chariots outside were on fire. We retreated just before hundreds more of their soldiers arrived. Our horses all cleared the fence and then gathered behind the rest of my cavalry, who had been firing arrows to cover our retreat.

We were all soon on our way back to Frome, with his daughter intact, apart from a few cuts.

Marcus rode alongside me.

"I have a bit of good news, Sir."

"Have you Marcus, what is your surprise?"

"Well Sir, while some of my riders were picking you and the ladies up. Some of my other riders were given a job."

"And Marcus, what job was that?" I asked.

"Have a look over there, Sir." He replied.

I could not believe it. There were sacks of corn, salt, rice... the list of items continued. There were even some sides of bacon!

"Well done, Marcus! This will help feed our men so we don't take all of Frome's food".

We arrived back just as the sun was rising. After ordering Sky and Mae, and not to forget Kuuli, to all go and get their wounds patched up. I then joined up with Deana and went to see Frome.

"I have brought your daughter back safe and sound, my friend."

"Thank you," replied Frome, "she has a few cuts, but none to be concerned about.

"You should see all the dead Egyptians that your daughter dispatched, I was glad to be on her side."

Then I collapsed. The sword cut across my side must have been deeper than I thought.

We all had treatment, and were told to rest for the remainder of the day.

Sky was in bed first; I was sitting on the side of our bed. I looked at Leon and Beaue, lying on the floor. They were really close to each other.

"Well, my love. I think our boy has developed into a loving adult. Did I tell you how I was with him when he was born? Just a bundle of fur." He was of course still just a big pup, all he wanted to do was play, eat and sleep. "Now he has a girlfriend to look after, and who knows, maybe we will hear the pitter patter of tiny feet one day. Well, ok, tiny paws."

"Go to sleep" said Sky, "we have all had a challenging day."

"Ok commander!" I replied, and slid under the sheets.

The next morning, I heard a knock on our door. I got up and opened the door, to see who it was. It was Lia.

"Come in," I said.

"I just wanted to let you know what is happening in my life." She explained.

"Great, I had been thinking of you". I replied

"First, I have told Marcus that I am giving Julius a chance to see if he is the same man I fell in love with back in Rome. Marcus is a wonderful and understanding man; he told me that he will wait and see how things work out. Second, Marcus is introducing me personally to all his men. This is giving me an opportunity to hear what his men believe about Jesus".

Sky was now sitting up in bed. "Morning Sky," said Lia, "can we have a chat later, if that's okay?"

"Sure, see you later," said Sky.

Chapter Three

Sand And Wind

The evening before our journey across the Nafud desert, King Frome had shown his appreciation by providing another banquet. A lot of wine was flowing, and a few of my men had already drunk too much.

I was watching a couple sitting not far from Sky and I - it was Deana and Kuuli. Deana was becoming very loud. Sitting opposite to her was Kuuli.

"Hey you!" Deana shouted, looking at Kuuli. "You look strong. How about an arm wrestle?"

"You're drunk. Go to bed." replied Kuuli.

"I am the strongest woman here," Deana started with a slight slur. She seemed to be getting fairly angry. "And maybe the strongest man also. Are you going to arm wrestle me? Or are you a coward?"

I doubted if Sky would agree that she was the strongest woman, and I would not be too quick to wrestle Kuuli. He was a tough target.

But the die had been cast. Kuuli was now up on his feet. No one calls him a coward. Deana was quickly up after him, standing opposite Kuuli and staring him down.

From my own perspective, I just wanted both of them to live. Both headstrong companions of mine were soon sitting either side of the table, with their arms locked.

Kuuli made the mistake of underestimating Deana, he mistook her for just a woman. When she, of course, was also a fine warrior.

In a flash, both arms were laying on the table, with the arm of Deana on top.

"One nil" I shouted, refereeing the match.

Kuuli did not make a second mistake, this time he used all his strength and soon it was the arm of Deana which was laying on the table, with the arm of Kuuli on top.

Sky looked at me and winked, as if to say 'it's all over now'.

I had been watching both of these strong people in front of me. Kuuli was a clever fighter, and cunning. Deana, on the other hand, was not particularly cunning, with her you get what you see - an athletic woman with very strong muscles.

"Would you like a bet on the winner?" I said, turning to Sky.

"Ok," she replied "If Kuuli wins, you will be my slave for a day."

"Then I will put my bet on Deana, with the same prize."

They both sat watching each other for a moment before the deciding round. Kuuli was cunning, but I had made my bet based on pure strength. They were both taking their time to place their arms down to begin.

Then, what Deanna had apparently been waiting for happened. Kuuli left his arm just on the edge of the table. In an instance, Deanna had grabbed the arm and slammed it down on the table before Kuuli had time to properly react.

Kuuli knew that he had at least lost to a clever and strong woman, one Kuuli could admire. Kuuli walked around the table to where Deana was standing in celebration.

"Well done," he said, patting her on the back, "we must have a drink sometime."

"Sure. Let's make it soon." replied Deana.

"So, my love," I said, turning back to Sky, "which day will you be my slave?"

Sky laughed, then turned to Deana.

Sky was staring at Deana. She was very annoyed, and it's definitely not good to annoy Sky. Sky had only ever lost one arm wrestling match, and that was not to a woman. Now this loud woman had beaten her friend, and former bodyguard.

"Deana! Do you honestly believe you are the best woman arm wrestler in this town?"

"My dear Sky," replied Deana. "In this town, I am the best arm wrestler, woman or man. As a woman, I am the best in the world"

"Well," replied Sky. "I have never been beaten by a woman either. Shall we have a match, to really see which of us is indeed the best?"

Deana smiled, then signalled to the chair opposite to her.

"Best of three takes the title for the best arm wrestler. Ok?"

Sky rose from her seat and moved to the seat opposite to Deana. I, being the loyal husband, moved to the seat beside Sky.

"Why are you sitting here?" asked Sky.

"Because, I am not only your husband, but also your coach."

Sky smiled.

"So, 'coach', what are my tactics today?"

"Well, my love", I replied. "The first push, I will leave you to decide."

I was about to watch two very strong women pitching their brains and strength against each other to see which one was the best woman arm wrestler.

Deana won the first push, by a wafer.

"One down, two to go, what tactics now coach"? Sky asked.

"Sky, my love, you will have to use the Beat, 'push me pull you' tactic."

Sky, looked at me with a puzzled look, and replied with a loud "What?"

I explained that she needed to use Deana's strength against her.

You give all your strength and push her arm downwards, then relax a bit, her arm will come up, but she won't need all her strength to push up, as you will be relaxing.

Then as both of your arms return to their start mode.

Deana, won't be using all her strength. That's the point that you give everything you have, slam her arm onto the table.

It worked like a dream.

"I don't believe it! I have never lost even one push before." Deana took a moment to psych herself up again. "Ok, the final one, let's see who is the best this time."

The two of them pushed to and fro for about half an hour. Finally, the skill and strength of Sky beat the total strength of Deana. The two women stood up, face to face, then Deana held out her hand.

"Well done, Sky, I concede, you are truly the best woman arm wrestler."

"I am not *totally* the best, someone not far from us beat me 3-0 not so long ago" she said, looking over at me, laughing whilst shaking Deana's hand.

I was now standing with my arms folded, I also had a smile on my face. What a woman!

"What was that noi…" I began, when all of a sudden, about twenty men came rushing into the room.

To my relief, it was just a group of tumblers.

"I presume that King Frome must have hired them for the entertainment," said Sky.

The group did various tricks, but the most impressive was five of the group who stood in a circle throwing a selection of knives and swords to each other. It was done with such perfect timing that the blades swirled and danced within a hair's breadth of each other, in a marvellous pattern, without making so much as a 'clink'.

As one of the acts caught a knife, then at the same time threw a curved sword into a target, a thought came to me. This act was so good with weapons, what if they were to attack us? I anxiously scanned the room. Most of the men were asleep or at least very drunk. I elbowed Sky.

"Be ready in case this group causes any trouble."

Kuuli was also concerned, he had seen me nudge Sky, to which he looked at me and nodded to show he understood.

That's three against twenty now, I thought. I got up and went to where Mae was sitting. Mae never drank wine so she would be able to join us if there was any trouble.

I looked around at our table, if there was an attack, the target must be one of us. King Frome was extremely drunk. He was face down on the table, next to him was Lia and Deana. I knew that Marcus also did not drink, as well as Quintin who was sitting next to him. I asked Mae, to tell all the aforementioned two to change seats, and sit as near to the King as they could, without raising suspicion.

I sat counting on my fingers, Kuuli, Lia, Myself, Sky, Mae, Marcus, and Quintin. That's seven, maybe Deana will be ok to fight, that's Eight. Eight against Twenty.

Then I heard a sound coming from under my legs.

I looked down to see where the sound was coming from, and there they were, the last two in my band that would thwart any attacks tonight.

"Come on you two, I have a nice leg of lamb for each of you."

Both Sky, and I were brushed aside as Leon and Beaue sprung up from beneath the table. Sky rubbed their heads as I searched for the meat.

"Ok Sky," I said, "Our band consists of more than enough power to take care of any problem, if our entertainment makes a move tonight.

We all, including Leon, were watching the tumblers. They were fairly average, except for the knife and sword throwing part.

I was told that they were due to perform for an hour, which is a long time for a tumbling act. Gradually the knife and sword juggling section appeared to be moving nearer to us.

"This is it," I whispered. "Be ready with your shield Marcus."

I was expecting one of the knife throwers to try and pierce the King's chest directly from the performing area.

Then it happened. All twenty of the performers charged!

But we were ready for the attack. We quickly gathered around the King and his daughter.

The fight was bloody, but short. They only outnumbered us two to one. They had no chance.

As the last attacker fell to the floor, the King raised his head, and asked for another cup of wine.

It was lucky that as soon as the fight started, Deana got her head together.

She was a bit drunk but as soon as she heard the clash of swords, the adrenaline must have kicked in and all effects of the wine evaporated. This girl lived to fight.

The following morning my army was all lined up, ready for our campaign against the Sassanid Empire. A hundred to each line, including humans, horses, camels and waggons. This was a massive fighting force. Heavy cavalry at the back, light cavalry riding up each side, the loaded camels with supplies were all in the middle and the foot soldiers were marching at the front.

As the Eastern Army marched off, I turned to King Frome and thanked him again for his help.

On a long journey like this, a large group like ours will often be targeted for their supplies - particularly food and water. Although there are few armies that would be strong enough to make an all-out attack on us.

I placed my light cavalry on our outside, as these guys were fast, and deadly with their arrows. I was also using them as Skirmishers, riding up and down the Dunes, checking for possible thieves.

It was nearly winter. Before me I could just see the red dust, which the desert was made up of.

Deana had informed me that the scouts she had sent into the desert had warned her that there were warnings of not only attacks on food, but also kidnappings.

"Well," I said to Deana, "I have done all you have asked to secure the train."

"I guess we'll just have to see if anyone fancies their chances."

Mae was riding her horse, with a camel beside her. The camel was packed with her belongings, as well as the remaining black powder. She was looking a bit down, and lonely.

Sky rode up alongside her horse.

"Are you ok Mae?"

"Yes."

"You don't look ok..."

"I just miss my husband, and my three children," Mae confessed, "it was over a year ago when I was kidnapped and taken to Serica[1]."

"Beat has promised to return you to your family, and he always keeps his promises! I want you to know that I am your friend, whenever you feel low, or just want a girly chat, I'm always here for you." Sky comforted her. "I'll let you in on a secret - as we are now close friends...

The other night, I saw Beat looking at a map, planning how to return

---

[1] Serica is modern day China

you to your family. After destroying the Sassanid Empire, we will continue into India, then travel through Serica (China), and drop south where we will cross the sea to your homeland. Then we may finally get to meet your family! I'm so excited to meet them, especially your children you keep telling us so much about."

"That would be amazing!" replied Mae. "I often feel the odd one out, as I come from so far away compared to everyone else".

"Well from now on, we will be the best of friends. You can come to me at any time, for anything."

The two women hugged each other - well, a one-armed hug seeing as they were both riding a horse. I had watched the proceedings, and I was sure that Mae was riding with more bounce in her saddle afterwards. That wife of mine has a heart of gold. Also, a sword of Iron and a fist of granite, bless her.

Deana, now joined me.

"There is a large tribe of Bedouins in the area," she said. "You had better ensure you double your guards tonight, and make sure that they are alert, or in the morning you may be missing... well anything"

I did exactly what Deana had suggested, after all Deana knew the area and its people. The following morning, I was awoken by Marcus and Quintin banging on my door.

Sky was already awake; she jumped out of bed and opened the door.

"I need to speak with the Commander," Marcus panted.

He sounded out of breath and for Marcus to be out of breath, he must have come to me in great haste.

I was now out of bed and sitting on our only chair - tents on a Campaign are not made for comfort.

Marcus approached and saluted.

"Sir, four of our Guards have been killed, and twenty containers of water are missing."

I was now fully awake, and furious! I had made a promise to my troops when I was first given command. I made this promise to my men that I would always try to bring everyone home safely, and here we were on our first night of camp and four of my men were already dead.

"Calm down my love" said Sky, she could see how angry I was.

Deana walked into the room.

"I did warn you last night about this possibility." Deana said as she walked into the room.

Was she winding me up? I thought. Sky saw the problem and quickly stood in front of me.

"Deana, this is not the time to use careless words! At this moment, my husband is very angry. Let us all wait until we all cool down and then we can start to plan what action to take."

I had been sitting with my head in my hands, I was so aggrieved, but I was also planning retribution. At last, I raised my head, and apologised to Deana, then gave Sky a hug and thanked her for preventing me from exploding.

"Do you fancy a bit of hunting tonight?" I asked, turning to Deana.

"Ok," she replied, a smile breaking her face. "How many of my men will you need?"

Sky looked at me knowingly, then turned to Deana.

"He has a plan. I can see by the look on his face."

Sky was right, my anger had cooled. It was now time for revenge! Payback time, for the lives of my men who died last night. I had planned to stay here for only one night, but necessity called for a second night's stay.

Last night, under the cover of darkness, local Arabs killed four of my men, and stole very precious water. Desert nights are cold and pitch black - true, the sky is filled with thousands of stars, but it is difficult to see in the darkness even so. However, a man's scent will still float about.

"Now who do we know who has an excellent sense of smell?" I asked with a grin on my face.

They both replied at the same time.

"Leon."

"And my Beaue, of course." Added Sky.

"Tonight, as soon as the sun disappears below the horizon, I will need forty of your warriors please Deana." I said, letting them in on my plan. "There will be Me, Sky, Marcus, Deana, and Kuuli. Plus of course Leon and Beaue."

"And what about us? Are you planning to have some night fun without us?" Chimed in a voice from the corner of the room.

They had entered my tent without me even noticing and had been standing in the corner listening to our discussion. Dash, I forgot Lia and Mae.

"Of course, he doesn't," replied sky.

"How could we leave you both out? I was just about to come and tell you both." I said, trying to save face.

"You little liar," Laughter spread across Mae's face. "You had forgotten us! And us being the best fighters here"

"Ok, so I forgot, but I had a lot on my mind." I confessed.

Then with a big smile across my face, I grabbed both of them around their waists and lifted them off the ground. I started to spin them around, when I saw Sky standing with her arms crossed, with a stern look on her face.

I quickly lowered Mae and Lia to the floor, and stepped back. Sky laughed, then through her arms around all three of us. Wow, I thought I was in trouble then.

There in the desert, the sun looked so beautiful as it set below the sands, and of course the sands of the Nafud desert were red, which seemed to shine under the setting sun.

I had decided to divide the group into two teams.

Team one: Deana, Lia, Marcus, and Kuuli (Mr Silent Killer). They had twenty of Deana's warriors with them. Sky had also lent them Beaue.

Team two: Sky, Mae, Quintin and I, plus the other twenty of Deana's warriors. Not forgetting Leon, the main man.

Team, one worked from left to right, while my team, team two, worked from right to left. The plan was that Leon and Beaue would track any thieves, while the rest of their team would follow and apprehend them.

It must have been two hours at least before Leon picked up a scent. That's all it took him, he was off. We all followed as quickly as we could.

Eventually we found Leon laying in the sand, waiting for us. He was maybe six feet, from a small group of men, wearing black robes. It looked like they were planning to attack two of my guards standing to attention beside a tree.

While I was deciding what action to take next, I heard a commotion, coming from roughly where the other team should be.

I waved my team forward, to engage with the would-be thieves. They were taken by surprise and all subdued in minutes.

I ordered both teams to return to my tent, with their prisoners. There they lay, twenty Arabs dressed in black robes, all nicely tied up.

"Who is your leader?" I asked

For a while there was silence. I had been thinking of the four young men who were killed the previous night. I ordered my men to take one of the Arabs and stake him out in the sand.

I then took a handful of Mae's black powder. I poured a thin line of the powder, from where I had been standing, up to and over the man's body.

I then got Deana to interpret what I was going to say.

"Listen to me, all my men are part of my family. They would die for me, and I for them. Last night four of my family were killed. In a minute, I will light this powder, it will burn up to and onto this man's stomach. At which point, his stomach and his insides will burn, slowly. Unless I get answers to my questions, each one of you will die the same way." I pointed at each of the Arabs laying in the sand.

I was no longer Beat, the shepherd boy, I was now able to deliver pain, the way a Roman can. I walked towards the start of the line of black powder holding the lit torch in my hand.

I stood there beginning to have second thoughts about being like a Roman, when one of the men on the ground shouted.

"I am their leader."

He spoke in perfect Latin.

I had him untied and taken to my tent. I provided him with food and drink. He said that he had not eaten for four days, but he would not eat before his men had eaten.

I was starting to have respect for this man. This is the attitude that I would expect from a true leader. I ordered that all his men should be released and fed.

He began to speak.

"My name is Aladdin. I am from the Nabatu tribe. The Nabatu worship many Gods."

"My people are Christians. We were driven away from the main body of our tribe, because we follow Jesus Christ."

"My people are starving and we have little water."

"We saw your army approaching, to us, we only saw the coming of food and water, the answer to our prayers."

"We are sorry that my men killed some of your guards. I am afraid they were driven to this by the need to get food and water for their loved ones. Commander, we will give your dead soldiers a proper Christian burial, it is the least that we can do."

While I stood thinking about this offer, Lia came across to me.

"Beat. I have been, with the support of Marcus, speaking with many of his legion. The four men who were killed, made a commitment to follow Jesus, the day before they were killed. I think it would be good to accept this offer."

I went with Aladdin to visit his village. I am a soldier, and I have seen some horrific scenes, but little compared to what we encountered at the camp of the Nabataeans.

Many people were starving, mothers were trying to feed their children but they had no milk.

Sick people were everywhere.

I grabbed hold of my head with both hands.

"STOP!" I shouted. "I have seen enough".

I turned to Marcus and Quintin.

"Return to our camp and bring a tenth of our supplies here."

"But sir," said Marcus, "what about feeding the army?"

I was now visibly upset.

"Marcus, take a look at these people, can we honestly leave them like this without trying to help? That wouldn't be very Christian now, would it?"

Marcus looked around, then he bowed his head.

"I'm sorry sir, I was wrong, we do need to share what we have with them."

"I am glad you agree with me Marcus."

"And also bring over all our medical personnel. And don't worry Marcus, I plan to replenish our food soon."

We fed and looked after the sick in Aladdin's village. The Nabataeans helped with the burial of my four dead soldiers. Then with heavy hearts, we left the Nabataeans.

"Now my dear friends, let's go and replenish our supplies."

I raised my sword and gave the command to march.

CHAPTER FOUR

WHAT IS WORTH MORE THAN GOLD?

Aladdin gave me two guides to lead my army to the main town of Nabatu. These were the people who drove Aladdin and his tribe away, with no food or water. This alone annoyed me. But there was also a second reason why I wanted to teach them a lesson.

This time I was wearing my Roman helmet. The Roman Empire was now a Christian Empire. So, I couldn't allow a small group of Christians to be treated the way that Aladdin's people had been.

I called Lia over.

"Lia, what does our representative for Christ think we should do to the savages who persecuted Aladdin's people?"

It did not matter what Lia thought. I planned to crush them. I had seen such horror in Aladdin's camp.

"Tell me my wonderful leader," Lia moved close to me, making me feel uncomfortable. "What do you believe Christianity is about?"

She paused for just a moment.

"Let me help you," she then said, before I had time to consider my response. "Do you believe that Christians should crush people who harm other Christians?"

Sky interrupted.

"Be careful what you say, my dear husband," Sky warned.

I was now a little confused.

"Yes. We should protect Christians and destroy anyone who would harm them."

"So, when Jesus told us to love one another, and to 'turn the other cheek', should we ignore this?" Replied Lia.

That's enough, I thought. When a good general is under pressure, retreat. So, I turned and almost ran out of the room.

"You were hard on him, Lia," said Sky.

"Was I? Or was I telling the truth?"

Everyone was ready to leave.

"Move out!" I shouted.

I rode up alongside Quintin.

"You have done well; I am pleased with how you have performed. Therefore, I have decided to reinstate you back to your role of general."

"Thank you, sir." Quintin replied.

"No need to thank me, you have earnt it. But… I want you to resolve the issue with Lia. Understand?"

"Yes sir" came his reply.

Sky, Myself, Beaue and Leon, have become inseparable nowadays. Beaue follows Sky around; Leon and I are always together; then of course, Sky and I are together most of the time. We are quite a formidable quartet.

As we rode, Deana rode alongside my horse.

"Beat, "have you noticed the colour of the sky?"

"Yes," I replied, "it's turning a dark red colour."

"That means that a sand storm is on the way." Deana warned.

I ordered everyone to halt, then positioned the heavy cavalry forward and put Marcus in charge of the cavalry. I instructed Deana and Kuuli to join me. Leon was beside me as always. I then commanded the rest of my army to take protection against the coming sandstorm.

As my heavy cavalry and I were about to leave, Sky rushed up to me.

"Why are you not taking me with you?" She asked.

"Because my love, I am putting you in charge here. I am relying on you to ensure that our main force survives the sandstorm. If this storm destroys our army and our stores, our chance of succeeding in our mission will be very low.

For once Sky did not argue with me. She understood the situation. She then turned to me and saluted

"Yes sir."

I love that woman so much.

"Thank you. I am off to retrieve supplies now. My trust is in you Sky." I turned my horse and galloped to the front.

There was Kuuli, Deana, the two scouts, and Leon. Not forgetting the cavalry of Rome's Eastern army. I hadn't really used them in this campaign yet. I think they were raring for action.

My plan was for the main formation to camp down, and protect themselves from the sand storm, whilst I pushed on fast with the cavalry, and hopefully we would be able to replenish our supplies before the sandstorm hit us.

I ordered the men to ride as fast as they could. The problem was that they could not ride too fast, as there were already sand particles circulating the air, making it hard to breathe.

Finally, I decided to leave Kuuli and Deana with Marcus, while I rode on ahead with Leon. I wanted to figure out if we could reach the town of Nabatu before the sandstorm hit my troops.

I had given Marcus orders that if the storm looked like it would hit before I returned, he must bed his command down to try to protect them from the sand.

Leon was having problems navigating the sand, his legs being shorter than my horse's legs, he sometimes sunk in up to his body. I tried to keep Leon in sight, but he often disappeared behind a sand dune.

I was getting worried, mainly because Leon had disappeared from my view, but also the sky was turning a dark red, and the wind was getting stronger. I slowed my horse to a trot, hoping that Leon would soon appear.

As the wind became stronger, and very noisy, my horse became frightened. He started to jump about, and stand up on his hind legs. I was having problems staying in the saddle.

Then it finally happened. I came off my horse and he galloped out of sight. I quickly got up off the sand and back onto my own two feet. Behind me there was no sign of my best friend. I really hoped he was safe. Everywhere was becoming dark and the wind was raging. Reaching the town of Nabatu was now impossible.

I took off my cloak and knelt down on the sand. I opened my cloak and covered myself with it. I attempted to anchor the cloak with my knees and my hands, trying to create a bubble which would store some oxygen, in case I got completely buried in the sand. Then it finally hit. I was thinking of Leon, all alone, he didn't have a cape. I was also thinking about Sky back with our main group. I was sure that the cavalry would be well bedded in by now.

The storm was now here. Everything else was forgotten. Inside my cape, I was in darkness. I could of course hear the wind roaring and the sand had nearly covered my body - I was being buried alive! No horse, no Leon, no cavalry, I was totally on my own, being crushed by piles of sand.

I was no longer kneeling, I had rolled myself up into a human ball, laying on my side. The air was running out. The weight of the sand was crushing me. 'What a way to die!' I thought.

All the people that I love started to run through my mind. 'I won't be able to hug my best friend again. No more kisses from Sky. Our dream of babies will never happen. I hope that she will survive and live a happy life.' I could feel tears running down my cheek. This would be where Beat the Shepherd boy ends his time on earth. Buried in sand.

Leon had been having problems running on the soft sand, and Beat was way out of sight. He stopped running and laid down on the sand.

Leon is an Anatolian Shepherd dog. This breed was bred to be independent, to be able to look after themselves, and make decisions for themselves.

Leon decided the best thing for him to do, as the storm was nearly upon him. Was to shelter behind a large rock, which had been uncovered by the wind.

The storm took maybe an hour to pass over before Leon dug himself out of the covering of sand. He jumped up onto the rock and surveyed the surrounding area. All he could see was sand. How would he find Beat? There were no tracks or scent to follow.

What Leon did know was that Beat had ridden north of where he was sitting, so he decided to search in that direction. Leon was very dehydrated, he needed some water, but there was none to be had. He knew that if he turned back towards where he and Beat had left the cavalry, he may be able to reach them and get a long cool drink of water. This action would delay his search for the man, who in his mind was his brother. They were not dog and master, they loved each other like brothers. Leon had no choice, he had to go over that rock and keep going forward until he found Beat, or he died.

Leon walked for maybe two miles before he collapsed. He lay there for a while getting a well-earned rest, but he knew that time was of the essence if he was to save his best friend. Again, he rose and walked on. Another mile passed by before he dropped to the sandy floor again. He was exhausted and desperately needed some water. But Leon had to continue somehow, he did by crawling, this large, strong, magnificent dog, was now nearing his end, crawling to save the man he loved.

Everywhere around, there was just sand. Finally, Leon collapsed for the last time, his strength had finally run out.

An hour later, Leon woke up to find he was laying on a cloak, with Marcus standing over him. Deana knelt beside him, offering him water. Leon had needed this sleep. Now, with a deep drink of refreshing water, he was standing, ready to continue his search.

Marcus rubbed Leon's head.

"No more running for you today my lad," he said. "Have a lift in our wagon and we will call you if we need you".

Leon was lifted up into the Wagon. Marcus then gave the order to gallop. The cavalry had bedded themselves down and survived the storm without any casualties. They were now in a race against time to save their Commander.

Deana had calculated how far Beat would have travelled before the storm hit. At this point, they let Leon off the Wagon. It was now time for Leon to do what he does best.

ॐ   ॐ   ॐ

I had once again almost given up on life. I was being crushed by the sand, dying for a drink and running out of air. I doubt if I would be able to survive another half hour. Then I lost consciousness.

I woke up, like Leon had, lying on a red cloak. I looked around hazily. Was I in Lia's Heaven? Or was I in Hades? Well, I understood that Hades is a very hot place, so out of the two, I must be in heaven. Mind you if this was heaven, it was not as nice as Lia had told me.

Then there was a large wet tongue licking my face, smothering me in drool. If this was one of those saints washing my face, they had better stop now. Then I saw it. Leon's head, followed by his large body. Marcus stepped between us,

"You two can have your hugs when you have both recovered," Marcus said sternly, looking down at me, "And that's an order!"

Deana came to visit me.

"You are a very lucky man," she said. "If Leon did not have the best nose in the world, we would never have found you". So once again, I owed my life to Leon.

It was two days before we both had recovered. Now it was time to visit a certain town. I sent the two scouts that Aladdin had lent me, to check out Nabatu.

They returned just after noon. The scouts had entered the town, and had time to look around. They told me that things were not that good. All the shops were closed, there were not many people around, most must have been in their homes. There were no guards anywhere in the town. I was told that it would be easy to take. I decided to have a look myself, as you never know, this could be a trap.

I left Marcus with the cavalry, and took Deana and Kuuli with me. Leaving a hundred men, a messenger and two medical personnel not too far away in case we needed back up. Of course, I changed from my Roman officers' uniform - it would have been a bit of a giveaway otherwise. All three of us walked into the town. We each entered from a different direction. Kuuli entered by the main gate - he was amazed as there weren't any soldiers to be seen - Deana entered by the south gate, while I skipped over a fence. We all met in the town square, which seemed a little eerie as there wasn't anyone there.

"We had better start to check the houses. The two of you check that big house over there," I ordered. I myself approached a house at the other end of the square. I quietly arrived at the back of the building, then edged my way around to the front door. There was this bad smell, it was very strong and started to make me a little sick. Now where had I smelt this smell before? I was trying to recall, as I let myself into the house. Ah, of course. In front of me were four beds. Three had dead people laying on them, the fourth was in a bad way. These people, who I had come to steal from, and maybe kill, to avenge Aladdin and his people, were mostly in the same condition as they were. I stood, feeling sick, and ashamed. I wished that Sky and Lia were there; they would have known what to do. Kuuli walked into the house. He came to report about the house where Deana and he had visited. I put my arm on Kuuli's shoulder.

"It's ok my friend. I already know."

I sent him back to Aladdin, to inform him of what we had found here. I leant over the young woman, who was still alive, although I was not sure for how long. I asked her who the town's leader was, and she told me how all the leaders had left.

"We ran short of food and water, so they took everything of value and left,"

I asked her how long ago they left.

"Two days," she whispered weakly, before collapsing and falling unconscious.

I felt my anger start to rise again. I sent Deana to take a hundred of my men after these people and told her to bring the two medical personnel to search for and treat sick people.

I sent for my cavalry to bring out the dead, those who were sick I had placed separately. I then gave orders for a search of the village for food or water. I had my cavalry dismount and help the people. When I first saw the people in their suffering at Aladdin's village, I had cried, and here again I felt tears running down my cheeks. I turned to look at my men, these were seasoned campaigners. They had fought many battles, killed and watched many people die. I would have thought these soldiers were hardened to scenes such as this, but I was watching these men crying as I was.

One of Aladdin's scouts informed me about an Oasis which could have water, as it was now early winter.

I asked how far this Oasis was from here and was told it was about a two-hour ride. I sent the scouts with two hundred of my cavalry, to collect as much water as they could. If they found a lot of water, not only would these people survive, but I could replenish our water supply.

It was now getting dark, but I had no intention of sleeping, there was so much work to do.

The moon had set, the only light now came from our campfires. I had given permission for my men to sleep in turns, half of my cavalry could sleep, then the other half.

The thing about night is that you can hear any sound. Ok there weren't a lot of animals here, but we could hear the odd insect. Then it came to my ears, the sound of hundreds of boots on the ground - men running towards us.

It was Aladdin and hundreds of his people. To my surprise they were carrying food and water.

Suddenly a pair of hands came across my eyes.

"Guess who!"

"There is only one woman with hands like this," I replied. I turned around with a smile on my face and pulled Sky into my arms.

"Enough of that," said another familiar voice.

"Hello Lia," I said.

Lia, tell me what's happening, had Aladdin and his men come to punish the people who did wrong to his people? The reply came from Aladdin himself.

"Beat, my friend, we are Christians, people may do us wrong, but we can forgive them. Jesus taught us to forgive our enemies."

I could not believe my eyes, we had laid the townspeople out, and now Aladdin's people were tending to them.

Then I was even more shocked, when I saw Aladdin people sharing the food which we had given them, we were not able to supply them enough food for themselves, now they were sharing what little food they had, with the people who had wronged them. It was heart-warming to watch.

The sun was rising when I heard a loud shout. My soldiers were returning from the Oasis. The people nearer to the riders were shouting

"Water! Water!"

I ran to meet them. Sky and Lia had beaten me there.

"Beat," said Sky, "They have brought gallons of water back with them".

It was amazing. There was enough water for both groups of Nabatu people, plus enough to replenish our supply of water.

"What is worth more than gold?" I asked Sky. Sky thought for a moment, then looked at me and smiled

"Cool, wet, water is the answer, my husband."

About noon, I saw more riders returning. Deana was leading, and she was shouting something. Sky and I raced to our horses; we were both anxious to reach Deana. I had a special reason, I wanted to meet the people who ran off and left their people to die. I had to ask them how they could be so cruel!

We soon met up with Deana.

"Do you have a present for me?" I asked.

"Did you doubt that I would catch them?" asked Deana, offended.

"Well, let's think. They only had two day's start on you… so of course you caught them," I said laughing.

Deana, winked at me, then pointed to the back of the cavalry.

"There are twenty cowards, with ten wagons of food. Plus another wagon full of gold and jewels."

"The funny thing is they never took any water with them. We found them lying beside their wagons, totally dehydrated."

"If they had left their jewels and gold and taken water in their place, then they may have escaped." I ordered some of my soldiers to erect twenty Poles, and tie these gentlemen to each Pole.

I waited until all the people had received medical attention, and had received food and water. Then I invited everyone to come to the town square, where the twenty town leaders were nicely tied to poles.

I had met up with Aladdin before the meeting, at the town square. I asked Aladdin what he wanted to do with these people who persecuted them because of their faith, and I told him that I planned to punish the town leaders myself.

Aladdin asked me to sit beside him.

"My friend," he scratched his head, "You are the emperor's instrument, with orders to make sure that everyone in the Roman Empire is, or becomes, a Christian."

"True" I replied.

Aladdin continued.

"Jesus Christ was persecuted and killed. Beat, did Jesus order all Christians to kill those who are not Christians?"

"I don't think so," I replied.

"You are correct. And because he didn't seek revenge, he now has thousands of followers. Think about it. We, the Christian members of the Nabatu tribe, are returning to this town. We will show that people of different religions can live together in harmony."

I thought to myself 'Lia should be listening to this', but silly me, she was standing not far behind me.

The twenty ex-officials of the town were given a chance to redeem themselves. They all had skills which could help the economy of the tribe. They were given jobs where they would help the tribe prosper.

Aladdin became the leader of the tribe, and he and his wife Lila would help the tribe to grow.

I checked on Leon, he had recovered well, he was hanging about with Beaue, so I knew he had recovered.

At dawn the following day, I gave the order for my army to move forward. We had a lot more desert to cross before we would arrive at the river which would lead us away from all this sand.

CHAPTER FIVE

CHARCOAL, SULPHUR AND POTASSIUM NITRATE

I continued to be amazed by the beauty of the desert. As the sun danced across the dunes, many different shades of red appeared. The red sands of the desert shone like a huge precious stone.

We had been travelling for nearly two hours. I made a good decision by crossing the desert during the winter months. The daytime temperature varied between 10°c to a high of 15°c. This made things easier for my foot soldiers - it can't be fun marching in the high summer temperatures. Also, the winter rains produce lush grasses to feed the horses and the camels.

We had about thirty miles to travel until we reached the stream, where we would turn north and finally leave the desert to head towards the Euphrates River.

I called Mae forward, it was time for her to depart on her mission, to collect enough chemicals to make the black powder. I was putting Mae in charge of three people, who would most likely still regard themselves superior to her and may oppose her orders. I had told each one of them about the mission, that I had put Mae in command. In the end, Mae would need to show her own leadership skills. There would be times when she would need to make quick decisions, which would require an instant response from her command.

She would also be taking Deana with her. I believed they would work well together. Next was Kuuli, I respected this man, he would also support her. Then she would have General Anthony. If she was truly a good leader, she would put Deana in command of the Ghassanid warriors, and General Anthony in command of the Alemanni warriors. Leaving Kuuli, to stay close to her in case of trouble. But that would be her decision to make.

I considered ordering all three of them to obey Mae, but that could result in a negative response to her command.

Mae rode alongside my horse and saluted me. I was about to laugh, as she was not one of my soldiers, but I managed to restrain my smile and returned her salute.

"Are you all prepared for your mission?" I asked her.

She now returned to the Mae that I know. Sitting on her horse looking relaxed, instead of answering me she asked me a question.

"Beat, are we leaving soon? As we are not too far away from the stream."

"Very true," I replied, "Take your command now, when you reach the stream, have your men wash themselves, then fill their containers with water before heading off to collect what you need. If a tragedy happens, and you are in danger of being defeated. Send Kuuli to find me, I'm certain he will succeed, then I will bring my cavalry to your rescue as fast as I can.

Eventually, they were all gathered, nearly two thousand warriors, with Deana, Anthony, and Kuuli, assembled at the front, waiting for Mae's orders.

I watched Mae ride up to her companions, she approached each one in turn, giving each one a high five, then saluting them. I think I was right to put Mae in command, she showed that they were all friends, with the high five, then took command with the salute. By returning her salute, they had accepted her leadership. I then spoke.

"I have one more young man joining this adventure."

I gave a whistle and two wagons drove towards the assembly.

"These are for your black powder, and someone else didn't want to miss the fun."

Leon jumped out of the front wagon. He ran up to Mae and sat just in front of her horse.

"That's the best he can do I'm afraid. He can't salute yet." Mae jumped off her horse and threw her arms around Leon. That's great I thought, I was the one who sent him - where's my hug? Leon returned to the wagon, and Mae and her command rode off into the unknown.

It was a day's ride to the stream. Well, I call it a stream, but it's really a river. I consider that a river is like the Euphrates River. Long, wide and powerful. Compared with that, this was a measly stream. However, it was enough to refresh all my men and livestock. We could also replenish our water supply. Not bad for a stream.

We were a lot slower than I expected in getting to the stream. Nearly a day and a half. I ordered my men to wash and refill our water supplies as quickly as possible, as I didn't want to be too far behind Mae, trouble could come at any time.

On exiting the Nafud desert, we would be entering The Sassanid Empire. From here to the Euphrates, and all the way to the city where The Sassanids ruled their empire - the great city of Ctesiphon.

I prayed that Mae was successful, and collected all the powder that we needed, and that they were all kept safe.

I was so worried that they may be attacked by the Sassanid army, before I could bring my army to their support.

Mae had let her command stay at the stream for as short a time as she could. She knew roughly where she would find the ingredients, she required to produce the black powder. There were some caves about half a day's ride where some of what she was looking for could be found.

While Mae's army was washing themselves in the stream, she noticed a group of ten strangers, fishing on the far side of the stream.

They of course had not carried a boat with them - it's not really the sort of thing an army would carry. A sword, spear, and a boat. No, that didn't quite have the right ring to it. She shouted to these men, with no response. 'What can I do to get their attention?' She thought… 'Aha!' She pointed to six of her archers.

"Each of you fire an arrow towards those men across the river." She ordered.

That got their attention. They immediately turned, raising their arms in the air, and started to shout something. Eventually they got into their boat and rowed across the stream to where Mae was standing.

As the fishermen left their boat and started to walk towards Mae, they were surrounded by soldiers.

"Leave them," Mae ordered.

The soldiers withdrew, leaving the fishermen wondering as to what to do. Mae waved them towards her, then asked them to have a meal with her.

These men had not eaten for many days. They spoke about how the game seemed to be very scarce and that they had been trying to catch some fish to feed them, for hours, without any success. Their families were starving.

Mae ordered one of the wagons to be emptied and had her soldiers load some food and water for their families. She told the fishermen to climb in the back, and thirty soldiers, with Mae, took the wagon to where they lived. There was so much excitement when they arrived, as Mae ordered her cooks to prepare a meal for the families. Mae watched as the children ate their first meal for ages, their faces all had a massive smile, Mae felt a warm glow in her chest.

Before she returned to her men, the fishermen gave Mae a warning. They told her that The Sassanids had a massive army to fight their major battles, but they had also left small detachments dotted around their Empire. These detachments were comprised of 20,000 soldiers. The really bad news was that one of those detachments was between them and the Euphrates River.

On hearing this, Mae ordered her men to return to the main body, with the wagon, immediately. She jumped into her saddle and her horse galloped as fast as it could. She needed to return to Sky, Lia and Marcus as soon as possible. Her army needed to be on the march, now, before The Sassanid detachment found Mae and her command. They were good fighters but would be outnumbered at least ten to one.

Mae had realised that speed was essential, in order to complete her mission. While her warriors were refreshing themselves in the stream, Mae gathered together twenty Ghassanid warriors. These were taught how to make charcoal, by burning wood, and had been given the task of producing the charcoal required to make the black powder.

Mae knew that sulphur could be found in various places, including hot springs and volcanoes and Potassium nitrate was found on cave walls. It was an accumulation of bat guano. Mae had been informed by the scouts, which Aladdin had lent to Beat, where both these ingredients could be found.

Mae sat on the bank of the stream, holding a meeting with Deana, Anthony, and Kuuli. She had to decide on whether to ride directly to the hot springs, and then to the bat caves. Or to split her troops by sending Deana and Kuuli to the hot springs, and Anthony and herself to find the bat caves. In the end she thought that time would be gained by splitting her troops. This was a big decision, because if one of these divisions failed to reach their target, she would not have the required chemicals to make the black powder. It was a gamble but one she believed was the right thing to do.

Both groups were given the instructions as to what to look for and how to gather it. Deana and Kuuli were given the task of collecting the sulphur, while Anthony and herself would look for the potassium nitrate in the bat caves. Each group was given one of Aladdin's scouts, to guide them and help find their allotted chemical.

Mae and her command had been riding in a straight direction, towards the Euphrates River. The bat caves were to be located five miles to the west. The hot springs were also on the west of the route, but another forty miles further. If Mae and Anthony managed to collect the potassium nitrate in a short time, they would be able to ride in pursuit of Deana and Kuuli, to support them with their collecting of the sulphur.

They all agreed that this was a good plan. At the designated spot, Mae and Anthony, with their warriors, broke away leaving Deana and Kuuli to continue north, to the hot springs.

Mae and her warriors made quick time and arrived at the bat cave within half a day.

"What a stink!" shouted Anthony. Anthony was brought up in the palaces in Rome. Only nice scented smells were allowed there.

"What kind of smell do you expect to come from a cave full of what is basically bat poo?" asked Mae.

The Alemanni warriors had no problem with the smell, they were more used to bad smells, than nice ones. There was one large entrance, but as they navigated the cave, it seemed to open out into many smaller caves. Mae split her men into two groups. Anthony led one group, these were ordered to search for older, dry and hard droppings at the bottom of the cave. While Mae and her group searched the area at the top of the cave.

Both teams had searched for over two hours without finding the poo that they wanted. Then a miracle happened. One of Anthony's men had walked into an unsearched part of the cave to relieve himself. Then low and behold, there it was, tons of guano. And it was all dry, the guano was exactly what they had been looking for. Mae gave her men a twenty-minute break, then away they went, gathering the poo off the walls and floor of the cave. By sunset, her warriors had collected enough to make the amount of black powder that Mae had planned to produce. Mae would have loved to let her warriors sleep until sunrise, then pursue Deana and Kuuli, but she knew that time was of the essence. She gave them two hours to rest, clean themselves, and be ready to leave. Cleaning themselves was a bit of a problem, as there were only a few muddy pools within the cave.

The sun had disappeared by the time her warriors were ready to leave. Mae had thought ahead and brought ten camels with them, these ships of the desert had no problem carrying the guano, and they never complained about the smell. Off they rode into the dark, where they soon disappeared out of sight.

Deana and Kuuli rode side by side at the front of the warriors. They were deep in conversation. It took one of their offices to enquire if they would be having a break, as the horses would need a rest. Deana turned to Kuuli and agreed with the suggestion that they should rest now, as there was little advantage in waiting until later. Kuuli nodded, and they ordered the troops to stop. Two hours later they all continued their journey in search of the hot springs.

When they arrived, everyone was amazed at the sight of the hot springs, but they were all equally as disgusted by the smell of the sulphur. They had arrived at dusk.

"It's too late to start our search tonight," said Deana.

She was correct, as it was too dark to search properly. After the day's long march, it was decided to let the men rest. They could start collecting in the morning.

Leon, who had been allocated to Deana's command, had been laying in one of the wagons. He had slept a lot, and was now well over his trauma in the desert.

He was back to his old self and ready for action. Leon could hear Deana calling him. His ears pricked up, and he left the wagon.

"There you are Leon," said Deana, "Would you like to join me in a bit of hunting?" Now hunting wasn't exactly one of our heroes' favourite pastimes. He preferred his meals to be brought to him, rather than having to catch it. So, he turned and jumped back into the wagon.

"Thanks," said Deana sarcastically, rolling her eyes. "Looks like I will be hunting on my own."

She couldn't take Kuuli as he would be running the camp. She sprung back into her saddle and rode off towards a distant oasis. The weather was warm for a winter's day. On arriving at the oasis, Deana jumped from her horse, and laid beside the pool. She felt relaxed and soon she was asleep.

People have good days and bad days. This was to be a bad day for her. In a country with miles of nothing, she had to be very unlucky to encounter army deserters. They were foot soldiers that had deserted from the Eastern army - too much walking and too little action. Roman soldiers do get paid wages, but the wagers are poor, most of their money is made up with what they can find on the battlefield - known as spoils of war. As soon as Deana fell asleep, they appeared from where they had been hiding, jumped on her and tied her up.

"I'll kill you all!" she screamed. It's true she would have. But that's if she was free. The ropes were a bit of a handicap.

After an hour had gone by, Kuuli wondered where she was. He asked a few sentries, but no one had seen her.

Leon had just poked his head out of the wagon, where he had been sleeping. When he heard her name, he jumped down from the wagon, and ran across to where he had heard Deana's name being called. He was soon standing in front of Kuuli.

"Have you seen Deana?" he asked. He had not been expecting a response, but Leon grabbed his arm as gently as he could and started to drag him towards the horses.

"What do you want? Have you something to tell me?" Now Leon was used to being with Beat, they understood each other. Trying to communicate with Kuuli could be hard work, thought Leon. Leon decided to change tactics, a more direct method needed to be used. He had managed to drag Kuuli as far as the horses, all he needed to do now was to get him into his saddle. Leon decided to use his strength to get him to understand what he wants him to do. So, he pushed Kuuli towards his horse, when he was rammed against his horse, the penny dropped.

"Oh, I see, you want me to get on my horse".

It's hard to explain exactly what Leon was thinking at this point. As soon as Kuuli was finally sitting in his saddle, Leon started to run in the direction that Deana had taken. The message had finally sunk in - Leon was leading him to Deana. Leon followed the fresh tracks that Deana's horse had made, and soon they both arrived at the oasis. When they arrived, there was no one there. There were signs of a struggle, but no people. Leon did not waste much time, he had sussed what had happened and was away, once again following the tracks - this time made by the deserter's horses.

They had travelled just over a mile, when they heard voices. They came from behind the sand dune in front of them. Kuuli told Leon to wait while he checked out who was making the noise. He crawled up the sand dune quietly. Upon reaching the top, he could see who the voices belonged to. Kuuli was shocked by what he saw. Below him was a massive army of Sassanid warriors. There were thousands of them. He could see six Roman soldiers, and Deana, being interrogated. He returned to Leon and told him what was going on. Kuuli wasn't sure if Leon understood, but Leon understood every word. Kuuli told Leon that this was what he was good at, he would silently creep into the camp when it became dark, kill any guards he came across, and rescue Deana. He told Leon to look after the horses. Leon had made friends with Deana; he had no intention of looking after the horses. Compared to me, Kuuli was an amateur, thought Leon, so he followed him into the camp of the Sassanids. The sun had disappeared, and the moon had now claimed the sky. Kuuli slipped into the camp, true to his nickname, he was silent. He had seen the area where they had been intercepted, and wasn't far away when, to his shock, he noticed the Roman soldiers nailed to wooden crosses. Rage overcame him, but he had to keep control of his emotions, as he had to find Deana.

Not far from the crosses was a large fire. He knew he had to keep to the shadows. Then he heard a crack as if someone had trodden on a dry stick, before Kuuli could react, numerous spears were pointing at his chest. He was quickly tied up and thrown into a large tent, not far from where the fire was still burning.

He lay in the dark, assessing his wounds, when he heard a sound.

"Who is it?" came a woman's voice.

"Deana, is that you?"

"Kuuli? What are you doing here? I left you in charge of the men."

"I had to find you." whispered Kuuli.

"Why?" replied Deana.

"Because I love you. Is that a good enough reason?"

For a while there was silence. Leon, who had been laying outside the tent, had followed Kuuli but kept a safe distance from him. Leon thought to himself 'lucky I am a more experienced fighter than these two.' He walked over to Deana and started to lick her face.

"Leon! How did you get here?", he gnawed through Deana's ropes in seconds, then went over to Kuuli. At first, he just stared at Kuuli.

"Ok." said Kuuli, rolling his eyes. "I know, you are the best." At that response, Leon chewed through his ropes.

"The best way to escape is this way" stated Kuuli. Then he saw Leon leaving the tent in the opposite direction.

"On second thoughts, let's follow Leon." They all followed Leon and were soon far from the camp.

When they arrived back at their camp, Deana immediately marched all her warriors to the hot springs. She realised that they needed to collect the sulphur as soon as possible, then catch up with Mae.

Mae and Deana met up as the sun began to rise. They had both managed to collect enough chemicals to make a lot of black powder.

Their next steps were to get back to the main army before the Sassanid soldiers arrived.

Deana, rode alongside Kuuli, and asked him about what he had whispered to her in the tent.

"In the tent?" said Kuuli, "I don't remember saying anything". Deana had heard him plainly, but she thought she would not pursue it here, it could wait. She smiled, and galloped up to the front.

CHAPTER SIX

LAST BATTLE BEFORE THE EUPHRATES

our hours later, Marcus was shouting.
"Here they come!"
I was so pleased. If Mae had met up with the Sassanid army, they would all have been dead, and there would not be any black powder. I gave the order to halt. Everyone needed to rest for a while. While the leaders and I met, everyone else could eat and relax. Mae explained about what her team had accomplished. Then Deana told me about what happened to Kuuli and her. With massive praise for my boy Leon. Once again, he had saved the day. Imagine what would have happened if Leon had not rescued them. Deana and Kuuli would have been dead, the Sassanid soldiers would have searched the area and found the Ghassanid warriors. Which of course they would have destroyed. Then they may have widened their search and found Mae and the Alemanni warriors. They would have all been slaughtered. Of course, all the chemicals to make the black powder would also be gone. Leaving me to attack the might of the Sassanid Empire, with just my army. Which, win or lose, would result in a lot of deaths. This was exactly what I was trying to avoid. Leon, words fail me to describe you, my friend. The only reward

I could give him was a large piece of meat and a big hug, but I felt like he deserved a lot more.

Well, my fellow officers, and friends. Our next mission is to remove twenty thousand Sassanid warriors from this war.

Sky was the first to speak.

"If we can get them to enter a valley, we can block the exit, then fire arrows at them."

"I like that idea, Sky, two things though… One, we will need to get them to charge into our target area. And two, do we have any idea where there is a valley with some kind of hills on each side?" I asked.

"At present, we don't unfortunately" replied Sky, "but let's send out scouts to survey the area and try to find one."

"I agree." Replied Lia and Marcus together. I thought for a while before replying.

"Ok, I will send out a small party to try and find a valley or something similar that could work."

"Marcus, please take twenty of the light cavalry, and search over an area of thirty miles. I will give you a week to locate a suitable valley, whether you find a valley or not, make sure you return after a week."

"Yes sir." replied Marcus.

"I want everybody else to prepare for a battle. Sharpen your weapons, practice, and prepare yourselves physically."

The meeting broke up and I went with Sky and the dogs back to our tent. Deana, on the other hand, went looking for Kuuli.

"Kuuli!" shouted Deana, "I want to thank you for risking your life trying to rescue me".

He was a shy hero, for years he had followed Sky, always in the shadows, protecting her.

"Maybe I tried, but I failed, didn't I?"

"Fail or succeed, you tried, many people would not have had the courage to even try" replied Deana.

Kuuli was now quiet, he did not know what to say. He would not agree that he was brave. He decided to change the subject.

"What do you think about the forthcoming battle?" he asked. Deana recognised what he was trying to do. She liked this kind of man. She remembered how he responded when she beat him at arm wrestling. He in fact praised her. Although she was never really sure if he had given his best.

"Well, my friend," replied Deana. "Would you like to share a flagon of wine with me, while we discuss it?".

"Where did you get wine?" asked Kuuli.

"There is no point in being a king's daughter if there are no perks," she replied, winking at him.

"Sounds good to me," he replied. Off they went to her tent together.

Quintin had been busy with his army duties, he had little time to see Lia, so he thought that this week could be his chance to get near her. Lia was practising her sword fighting skills with Mae. When they finished, he asked Lia if they could have a chat.

Lia was aware that she had told Quintin to court her, so she had no option than to agree.

"Yes Quintin, it's time we found time to talk. We can go to my tent." Quintin apologised for not being able to see her of late and reminded her that she had told him to court her.

Lia said that she understood that they are in a war setting, and romance would be difficult. She also told him that if he really loved her, he would make time for little things. Quintin didn't understand.

"What do you mean by little things?" he asked.

"Well, if you don't know, then maybe we should not be together." This riled Quintin.

"Maybe you haven't noticed, but there aren't any museums, or art galleries, or nice places to eat out here."

"I never mentioned any of those things. I said little things".

"Little things…" he bent down and picked up a stone. "Here you are. This is a little thing."

Lia smiled.

"You picked up that stone, where if you had looked through the eyes of love, you would have seen that small flower, maybe two hands length away from that stone."

"I am sorry Quintin, I don't want to see you any more, I will take my chance back in Rome as to what the true law of Rome regarding our marriage is."

With that, Lia pushed him out of her tent. Mae had been standing nearby her tent, and watched Lia push Quintin out.

"Can I give you a tip?" asked Mae.

"What?" replied Quintin.

"If I were you, I would give up on Lia. You have no chance there, find yourself someone else". Quintin's response was to storm past her.

"And that's goodbye to you" Lia mumbled. Mae smiled, then asked Lia if she was ok. Lia asked Mae to come into her tent.

"To be honest Mae, I feel relieved to see the back of him."

"I thought that you were both going to be married back in Rome?" Lia sighed.

"It's true. We both thought that we were in love, and my parents gave him permission to marry me. It was a lot time ago and I now believe that, as far as I am concerned, it was just a crush."

"Lia, what will happen when you return to Rome? Will the law of Rome make you marry him?"

"Maybe," replied Lia, "but I am hoping that the Pope will overrule it. Anyway, I won't have to engage with Quintin until then, and I plan to tell Marcus everything."

A week went by. No sign of Marcus. I was now getting concerned, Marcus was my top general, he would never be late unless something bad had happened. I wanted to take some of my soldiers and search for him, but the problem with being in charge is that I am needed with my army.

"I will go," suggested Sky. I thought for a bit, then gave her the ok. I told her to take Lia with her and twenty of the light cavalry, but ordered her not to leave until Marcus was two days late.

Mae was busy making the black powder, but when she heard trumpets blowing, she rushed outside her tent, where she saw Marcus returning. He was a little down, because he had returned late. He found me as soon as he could, he saluted, then apologised for his late return. There was good news and bad news. The good news was that he had found a valley. It was ideal for my trap. Narrow with steep walls on either side. The bad news was that about eight thousand Sassanid soldiers were split off from the main camp and were camped about a mile from the valley. Somehow, we needed to get all twenty thousand soldiers inside the valley.

"Leave it to me, Marcus. I will have a think and find a solution. I believe Lia is looking for you.

I chatted to Sky, Mae, Deana and Kuuli. We finally came up with a plan. Anthony, Sky, and Lia, would lead ten thousand of my heavy cavalry. The plan was for Sky to get the Sassanid commander to believe our ten thousand soldiers were about to attack their eight thousand soldiers.

"How can we make their commander believe we are about to attack?" asked Sky.

I looked at my warrior woman and smiled.

"All you have to do, my love, is to take your command within a mile of the Sassanid main camp. They will have their sentries stationed behind the rocks and trees. As soon as you are seen, they will report to their commander, he will panic and send all his men immediately to attack your command."

"I guess that could work," replied Sky. She gave a quick wave and disappeared before I could protest. That woman of mine. She would be on her horse already. Shame she never waited for me to tell her what to do when she was being pursued by the Sassanid army.

"Leon!" I shouted, "Stop Sky, I will be with you as soon as I can."

Sky was fast, but not in the same class as Leon. He was in front of her horse in minutes. Her horse started to panic when Leon arrived. Horse's do get attacked by wolves, a big dog like Leon would startle a horse. Although Sky, being an excellent horsewoman, soon had it under control. She looked down at Leon and asked what he wanted. By then I had just about arrived. I was puffing and blowing, I am fit but I'm more of a distance runner - I don't normally have to run that fast. There I was, leaning against Sky's horse, hoping it would not move and leaving me lying on the ground.

"Beat, what do you want? You are puffing like an old man". At this point, I noticed ten thousand soldiers looking at me. I suddenly found some new energy as I sprang to attention. Then, looking up at Sky, I told her that if she had waited a bit longer, I would have told her what to do when she had twelve thousand Sassanid soldiers pursuing her, without having to chase after her. Sky realised her mistake and used her female tricks again.

"Well, my love, I did rush out, but there was a reason."

"And that was?" I asked.

"Well, I wanted to see you again before I left."

I stood there unsure how to respond to that. Should I reprimand her in front of her command, or pretend nothing had happened.

"Well, Commander Sky, when you have the rest of the Sassanid army following you. Charge towards the eight thousand camped near the valley. As you are approaching them, split your riders, so they pass either side, and ride like mad into the valley. When your command has exited the valley, Mae will use her black powder to cause an explosion, and rocks will block the end of the valley. At that point, the majority of my army will then start to enter. My archers will be stationed high up the slopes, ready to fire down on the Sassanids. After their commander can see they have no chance to escape, I will speak with him. Sky lent down to where I was standing and put her fingers under my chin, looking me in the eyes.

"You are not just a pretty face," she said. Now I could hear lots of laughter. I slapped her horse and told her to get out of here, which she did, still laughing.

Everything went as planned. Sky led her command near to where Deana and Kuuli were captured. Very soon she heard the sound of lots of horses riding at speed towards her. She gave her soldiers the order to gallop towards the valley. As the smaller group of Sassanid soldiers came into view, she ordered her riders to split and ride around the enemy, into the valley.

As Sky and her rider were just over half way into the valley, she started to wonder if the valley had an exit. With twenty thousand soldiers pursuing her, she was relieved to see the end.

As the last of her riders passed out of the valley, there was a loud explosion. Followed by tons of rock tumbling down and blocking the exit. There were clouds of dust everywhere. As soon as all the Sassanid soldiers were in the valley, the whole of Rome's Eastern Army moved to block the entrance. I had one of my soldiers raise a white flag.

I met up with the general of the Sassanid soldiers, a mile from the entrance to the valley. He was a mature man; I would put him about fifty years of age. He had grey hair, with the look of a man who had been in many campaigns.

"My name is Commander Zug."

"My Name is General Shahpur," he replied. Well, you can see the situation, I said. "I could kill every one of your men, but I don't want to." I let that sink in for a moment then continued. "I wear a Roman uniform, but I don't have a Roman heart. I have no wish to slaughter your men, but I can't let them roam free to attack my army at another point. In the past I have had defeated soldiers' thumbs and toes cut off.

General Shahpur, started to speak.

"I have fought many battles, having only lost a few. I have met many leaders of men; Generals, Commanders, et cetera, but I have never come across a leader, who first tricked his enemy, trapping them, but was willing to show mercy, rather than slaughter them. Why is this?"

Leon was standing next to me. I put my arm around his neck and gave him a big hug.

"General, see this dog. He is strong, and intelligent, He is everything a general should be. He has saved my life more times than I can remember. Yet he doesn't kill for the sake of it. Yes, he has killed, but not out of hatred. He only kills out of necessity. If he is fighting a battle, arrows flying everywhere, swords slashing to and fro, he has to kill in that situation. But in a situation, when I have told him to take out a sentry, rather than kill him, Leon will take hold of his throat and gently squeeze until the sentry loses consciousness. I have learnt from him. Generals send men to kill and soldiers do what they are ordered to do. Your soldiers are in this valley waiting to die, not because they wanted to be there, but because you ordered them. So, really, I only should have you killed. Tell me, general, what should I do in this situation?"

The general threw himself to the ground.

"You are right. Or maybe I should say, your dog is right." I was fooled into charging after your small detachment of cavalry, then I rushed into this valley without checking that my men could get out at the other end. Of course, they are now waiting to die because of my orders. Please, kill me and let my soldiers go free."

"General, I have a generous offer for you. I am taking my army to kill or capture your emperor. I will let your men live, *IF* they do not involve themselves in the battle to take your emperor."

General Shahpur, smiled. "I accept your mercy. I, and these Soldiers of mine, will make camp in this valley until you have either killed our emperor, or you are defeated." I held out my hand to him, he grasped my hand to seal the agreement. Then he laughed. "I think we hate our emperor more that you, he is an evil, murdering, lying, tyrant. And yet we must serve him. I hope we meet again after you have won."

We said farewell to the general and rode away heading towards the Euphrates.

We spent two days at the great river, preparing for the main battle. Then we followed the river south, until we turned north along the river Tiber. It wasn't that long before we could see the spires of the capital. The city of Ctesiphon. My army camped around the city to enable us to stop any food going in. I was sitting on my horse watching the sun rise, when something happened that totally shocked me.

"Thank God!" I shouted.

"And which God is this?" It was Lia.

"Lia, how many Gods are there? Well, Gods that have died, then come back from the dead."

"Only one."

"That's the one," I replied.

"So, what are you thanking him for?"

"Our enemies are safe behind that massive stone wall. Well, I say safe, but Mae has some plans to bring the wall down. Anyway, they are sending their army out to fight us on the plain. No one does that by choice. Roman soldiers have spent most of their lives training and practising battle moves. No one fights a Roman army on the open plains."

"I expect it's because they outnumber us two to one."

"Will that make a difference?" asked Deana.

"No chance." I replied.

I galloped back to my troops. My plan was the same as always. At the centre of the formation would be my foot soldiers. These men hadn't done any fighting yet, they would be dying to get some action. My light cavalry would ride up and down the flanks firing arrows into the enemy riders. My heavy cavalry would position themselves and wait for a given signal to smash into the back of their foot soldiers and any cavalry they have.

"Can I have a word with you please Beat?" asked Mae.

"Is it about the Black powder?"

"Yes," replied Mae. "This is a bag of black powder, I have added lots of small shards of metal and when I add a small piece of string, and tighten the bag, we have a small bomb. You can give them to your light cavalry. They can get their bomb lit, ride up close to the enemy and throw their bombs. It will also make their horses panic."

The battle worked like a dream. It was over in six hours. I saw one of my soldiers kill the emperor and as he fell to the ground, his crown slid off his head onto the grass. Immediately the man jumped off his horse, picked up the crown and tucked it inside of his tunic. I ordered five of my men who were carrying bows, to fire towards the soldier, who I pointed out. I told them I just wanted to attract his attention, not to kill him. The third arrow hit his shield and he turned to the direction the arrow came from. There I was, his commander, looking sternly at him. He almost collapsed onto the ground as if an arrow had sunk into his heart. I then sent a rider over to collect the crown.

"Give that man this bag of silver," I said, "he deserves something for finding it."

The other success was Mae's Bombs. A rider would collect a lit bomb from Mae, ride as close as he could to the enemy, throw the bomb, then immediately turn his horse round and retreat before the bomb exploded.

The explosion caused horses to bolt, but most damage was done when the small metal shards hit their soldiers, causing massive harm.

Then came the part which I personally hate. Counting our dead. I had done all that I could. Many had died, but not as many as there could have been.

Next, I had to meet up with the royal family, along with close friends and relatives.

I decided to leave it for a day before entering the city. However, before I entered, I sent in three legions of my best troops. They were under orders not to kill, rape, or steal anything, or they would be severely punished. I wanted them to ensure that the city had settled down, and everyone was ready for my arrival.

CHAPTER SEVEN

WHO'S A DADDY?

S ky and I were lying in bed. I was tired but my head was running on overdrive.

"Sky," I said, "Do you think Beaue has been acting differently of late?"

"Typical man," was her reply. "you men don't understand anything about us girls". I was now completely lost.

"What are you talking about?" I asked.

I turned to Leon and asked him if he knew what was up with Sky. That was stupid of me as Sky overheard.

"What am *I* up to?"

"Sorry Love, I just don't understand what I said wrong."

Sky smiled, then she slipped her arm in mine.

"Let me tell you about the birds and the bees," she said. "Leon, is going to be a father!"

"Do you mean that Beaue is pregnant?"

"Well done! I think you had better buy some presents," said Sky.

I gave Leon a big hug.

"So, you are going to be a daddy!" I said to him, "Let's see if I remember. I believe your mum took 63 days for her to have you. Also, a mother Anatolian shepherd dog can give birth to between ten to fifteen pups. It will feel like I'm back home when there are little pups running around everywhere." I paused for a moment with sudden realisation. "Hang on… tomorrow we are to enter the city."

Sky once again put her arm around my shoulder, "Beat, my love, there are at least thirty-five days to go until the birth."

I relaxed a little.

The following morning, I selected Mae, Sky, Deana, Kuuli, Marcus, Quintin, Lia, and Anthony to ride with me at the front of the procession. I could not take the whole of my army into the city as that would seem unfriendly, and I wanted to enter as a friend. Therefore, I just took one hundred of my foot soldiers, fifty of my heavy cavalry and fifty of my light cavalry.

It was strange, we had just destroyed their army, but the people were lining the streets and cheering us. I then remembered how General Shahpur reacted when we told him we were going to capture or kill their emperor.

We dismounted outside the palace, then were approached by two guards, who asked me for my weapons. I chose to see this mistake by the guards as funny. There was me, with my army which had just conquered their city, and they were trying to stop me entering the palace while armed. When twenty sword blades pointed at them they realised they may have made a bit of an error and withdrew.

The palace was impressive. Since joining the Roman army, I had visited quite a few palaces but this must have been the most amazing. Everywhere there was gold and precious jewels used in the décor. As I walked into the main hall, I was still gazing around the walls and ceiling, when I heard a voice. Regaining my attention, I looked to where the voice came from. There, sitting on a throne of Gold, encrusted with rubies and emeralds, was a beautiful dark-haired woman. Beside her and along both sides of the hall were her, what we in Rome would call, senators. She had reserved the front row in the centre of the hall for my entourage and I. The throne overlooked where we would be sitting, leaving her appearing to be the one in power. I told Sky and the others to wait where they were. I then walked slowly towards the front of the hall whilst stroking my chin. On reaching the front of the hall, I climbed the steps up to the throne. Then standing behind the throne, I leant forward, and asked her why she was sitting there. She, to my surprise, ordered two of her soldiers to come out from behind a curtain and cease me. What fools. The first soldier died with my sword in his stomach, the other one lay on the floor with Sky's arrow in his heart.

For a moment I wished that Leon was with me, but I had left him back at camp with Beaue. He would be with me in future but I understood that he would now also have fatherly duties too.

Sky and Deana were now standing on either side of this woman, holding her tight. I approached the official sitting nearest to the throne. I pointed my sword at his stomach.

"Would you like to tell me what is going on? I have had a tiring few days and I am starting to get a bit angry." He asked if he could speak with me in private. I agreed and we went to a nearby room. There he told me the truth.

"The woman on the throne was the wife of the dead emperor. She was trying to continue as the new empress. She had locked up his step daughter. I say step daughter, she was the daughter of a woman he married last year. He killed the woman's husband in order to marry her, then six months later killed her, in order to marry the current empress. He was an evil man. The people hated him, that's why they cheered when you rode through the streets."

I called Quintin forward.

"Yes sir?"

"Quintin, go with this man and bring the princess to me." I then turned to the official and asked him if there was a more suitable room to meet. He replied that he would organise this and send someone to fetch me.

Two hours later, we were all sitting in this luxurious room. As the Princess was female, I brought Sky, Mae, and Deana with me, and I also brought Quintin. Our hosts surprised me by serving wine and various delicacies. As we ate, we chatted. I, of course, started the conversation. I asked the princess to tell us her story. This she was more than willing to do.

"Four years ago, the emperor wanted to marry my mother. She was happily married to my father, but the emperor had him killed, then forced her to marry him. I, my mother's daughter, was treated like a slave. I was used as the emperor's servant, serving his meals, running his errands, that sort of thing. Eventually, he planned to marry me off to some wealthy merchant. He bullied me and my mother. She wanted to kill him. One night, after he beat me, she tried to stab him. But unfortunately, she failed and was beheaded. He starves the people and rules by terror. I hate him, and the people hate him. Your army taking the city and killing the emperor is the best thing to happen here. Our biggest fear is that the Roman Empire is known to also rule with harsh laws, followed by cruel punishment if their laws are broken."

Mae sprung up from where she was sitting. Then started to speak to the princess.

"You presume that we are all Romans, just because we march under a Roman Eagle. In this room, only Quintin is truly Roman. The rest of us are from other countries. Beat, our Commander, was born in Helvetia. Princess Sky was born in the Alemanni Tribe, in Germania. Deana, is a Ghassanid Princess. None of us live by Roman ethics. So have no fear. Commander Zug, is a fair and just leader. So, listen to what he has to say." Then she sat down.

Wow, I thought, that was a hard act to follow.

"Princess, please find us somewhere to spend the night. In the morning I would like to spend time with you before I decide what I am to do with the Sassanid Empire."

"I will see to this immediately," replied the Princess.

"Quintin, please inform the officers of what is happening. And send Leon and Beaue, up to wherever I am." I ordered, then he turned and left.

Early the following morning, I met up with Quintin. I had something important to tell him. The two of us met up under a large palm tree. We sat together on a grassy bank.

"Quintin, when I first met you, you were in an argument with Lia. She is a good friend of mine and I became very angry. Lucky for you I am not a true Roman, or you may have been dead. I am glad that I managed to control my temper that day, because having got to know you more, I respect you as one of my top officers." I told him honestly. "I understand that Lia is now avoiding you and refusing to even talk about marriage. In fact, she spends a lot of time with Marcus now-a-days. Marcus told me one evening, that you only wanted to marry Lia, for fame and wealth, not love."

"Yes sir, that is true, I still care about Lia, and I am happy that they are getting on well together. It was hard at first but I understand now that I was wanting to marry her for the wrong reasons." He admitted.

"Quintin, I have a request. I want you to be involved in the reconstruction of the Sassanid Empire." Quintin looked very surprised, even shocked.

"I will do whatever you wish sir," was his response.

"Thank you, Quintin, I will inform you of our first meeting."

I then hurried over to my meeting with the princess. What a fool, I never asked her name. I was led to the room where we were to meet. As soon as she entered the room, I saluted her and introduced myself.

"Good morning, I am Commander Zug."

"My name is Princess Shirin," she replied.

"Today, Princess, I would like you to take me on a tour of your city please."

"It will be my pleasure," she replied. "Shall we use the state coach? Or ride our horses?"

"I think it would be good to ride, and maybe not wear our normal clothes."

"Where would you like to go Commander?" asked Princess Shirin. "Would you like to visit our monuments? They are many thousands of years old."

"First, you can use my name, my name is Beat, you can drop the Commander."

"Then please call me Shirin. But the question is the same - where do you want to go? Or rather, what do you want to see?"

"To be honest, I want to know more about your people, not about those who are wealthy, but those who have little, who may be struggling to feed their families each day."

"I am pleased to hear that you care about the poor, I know just the place we need to visit."

In no time at all, we arrived at a market, I believe it was known locally as a 'bazaar'. Many people were purchasing various goods. But everywhere, I could see beggars and people only able to buy small amounts of food for their families.

"I presume that these are the people that I was talking about wanting to see?"

"Yes," replied Shirin, "many of these people are starving and many are sick, but can't afford treatment."

I began to notice people of both sexes, old and young, coming towards us.

"They are after our horses," shrieked the princess.

I pulled the horses together and drew my knife from my belt. I ordered the princess to get behind me. Then I saw that she was another of these warrior women, that I keep making friends with. I even married one, which was one of the best moves I had ever made, despite the odd bruise, or bump. The princess also had a knife and was now ready to protect her horse.

"I don't want to worry you, but we are two against maybe fifty starving people."

The princess agreed, but at the same time refused to let her horse be killed. For once I was lost as to what action we should take. Then I heard a loud bark.

"That sounds like my Leon!" I told the princess. But he was back at the palace, so it couldn't be him. Then I felt a big animal brush against my leg. I looked down and tears of joy started to run down my cheeks.

"Leon, how did you get here?" My boy is a great actor, he was standing next to me, letting me rub his side, then he moved in front of us. He rose to his full height and started to show his teeth and barked. The crowd that was about to tear us apart to get to our horses, began to panic, and melt away down side streets.

"I can't say I blame them." I grabbed the arm of the princess, and told her to get on her horse.

"Let's get back to the palace." Two horses and my Leon hastily exited the bazaar.

How did Leon, once again, arrive in time to save my life? Well, he heard us leaving the palace. Now Leon is not only very strong, he is also very clever, unlike me. He decided to follow us, he knew that dressed as we were, no one would recognise us. Not many people knew the princess anyway, she has spent most of her life locked inside the palace. Anyway, he followed us, and as he expected, I was in trouble again.

I gave Leon two chunks of; I think it was camel. Anyway, he had one for himself and he took one to his missus. The princess and I went into a large banqueting room. I started to talk to her about my plan for the empire after my army and I left. I told her that I was forming a group to prepare for the future of the Sassanid Empire. I asked her if she would like to be part of this planning group. She jumped at the chance. I told her that I planned to stay here, until Beaue and Leon's pups were born, it would be too bumpy in a wagon for an expecting mum. We would all meet up for our first planning meeting tomorrow.

"Sorry, I would like to ask you… do you have a religion?" I asked

"My parents were both Christians, I would say I am also a Christian, although I often wonder why my Christian parents were both killed. I thought that Jesus would protect them."

"You need to speak with Lia, but I can guess what her reply will be. She will tell you that being a Christian, will not necessarily give you a long life in this world. It will give you everlasting life in Heaven." I said "Oh, I almost forgot, before I leave, I have a message for you from one of my generals. His name is Quintin, he would like to meet you this afternoon, is that possible?"

"Is he the tall one who I saw when we first met?"

"Yes, that's him. I did not like him when we first met, but since then I have grown to respect him, as a warm and kind hearted man. He is one of my top generals and I have big plans for him.

"Well then, I guess I had better meet him. It should be an interesting afternoon." She replied.

"I have to go now, see you at tomorrow's meeting. Ten o'clock in this room."

I had to rush away, as I hadn't told Quintin of his date yet.

I was glad to get back to my Sky that evening. I told her all about the day's adventures. Ok, so I was behind my shield when I mentioned the escapade at the bazaar. As it was, she had known that Leon was following us, she had watched us leave, with Leon not far behind. She knew that with Leon following, we would be ok. Also, it saved her having to follow herself.

The following morning, there was Sky, Mae, Lia, Deana, Quintin and I. Then last but not least Princess Shirin walked into the room, looking every bit a princess.

I informed the meeting that I planned to leave the Sassanid Empire in three months' time, or after Beaue had given birth, whichever is the earliest. I then told the group (I hate the word 'committee'), that when we leave, two people, whom I would appoint, would rule the empire. I never said on behalf of Rome. Simply this was because my orders were to kill or capture the emperor, and teach the Sassanid people a lesson, so they don't cause problems for Rome again. There was nothing in my orders about making them part of the Roman Empire.

The meeting was about delegating various jobs to the members. When the meeting broke up, everyone was talking about who would be the two people that would be appointed to rule the empire.

When we were back in our room, Sky rushed me onto our bed and rammed my arm up my back into an arm lock.

"Ok honey, who are the two people that will rule the Empire?"

I was a bit stronger than this beautiful woman, so it wasn't long before she was laying on her back, with me on top.

"If you wanted to know my love, you only had to ask."

"I hope it is not us," she replied. "This place is too far away from my family."

"No, it's not us." Was my reply.

Then she started to torture me, so I would give in and tell her who I planned to make the emperor and empress. First her arms were used to hold me, then her lips were used. I can never hold out for long with her interrogation tactics.

"Ok, it's the princess,"

"Well, that's no surprise, but who will be the emperor?"

"I can't seem to remember at present, you may need to interrogate me a bit more."

She gave me the stare that means, 'tell me now or, I won't cook your dinner tonight.'

"I plan to make Quintin the emperor."

"Really?" she replied, surprised "I thought he was trying to marry Lia?"

"He was, but he wasn't truly in love with her, he just wanted a high position and money. As an emperor, he will get both."

"Are you going to make them marry? They aren't in love with each other, that would be cruel."

I hopped off the bed and stood to attention.

"May I introduce you to our own Cupid." Sky laid back on the bed in fits of laughter.

"Ok, where is he then?" I looked at her, and pretended to fire an arrow. That did it, she was now laughing so much, she could not even speak.

Later, I met up with Quintin. I wanted to have a man-to-man chat with him. Not as a superior officer. We met up at a place where we could share a bottle of wine, but this place didn't sell wine. I am not sure what it was, but it was strong. I asked Quintin about his relationship with Lia. He replied honestly, he told me that it was over. He was only with her because her parents were wealthy and senators. I then asked what he thought of Princess Shirin. At this question, he became rather shy.

"Well sir, we spent time together yesterday afternoon. We got on well together. She has had a difficult life, both of her parents were killed. As a princess, she was more like a prisoner. I began to realise that the life I have been living is far better than the one she has lived."

"As a person what do you think of her?" I asked.

"She is beautiful, caring, gentle, but at the same time she won't listen to fools. Also, she has a heart for the poor, and the helpless."

"Quintin, I would like you to spend as much time with the princess as you can over the next three months. I am putting you in charge of her security."

"Yes sir," he said formally, but I could see a slight smile on his face.

I could not get back to Sky quickly enough. I walked into our lounge, with the smile on my face of a man who had just done something amazing.

"Ok," said Sky, "What have you done?"

"I haven't done much…"

"With that smug look on your face, you have done something," replied Sky. She was now within striking distance.

"Well, my love, you can call me Cupid if you want."

"I often call you stupid, what is different today?" she joked.

I grabbed her and gave her a kiss.

"You are fully aware that I said Cupid… I, Beat, have gotten Quintin interested in the princess."

I had given the princess and Quintin the responsibility to monitor the poor and evaluate what their needs were. Sky and Deana, were to research the Sassanid Empire: what allies they had, who their enemies were, what food they produced, et cetera. Mae and Kuuli were given the task of looking into the finances of the empire. I added Kuuli because I needed to evaluate the work.

I had been concerned about my plans to journey through India and Serica. They were both very large countries - could my foot soldiers walk that far?

Then a plan came to me. We had maybe two months left before the birth of the pups. I would get all my foot soldiers trained to ride a horse and to fire arrows. Then if we found some who were very good, I would create a new regiment. The others could ride, but fight in formations on the ground during a battle. I asked Anthony to arrange this. I did not want him to do the training, just delegate.

Time seemed to fly by. Beaue was almost at her due date. Leon was getting nervous, I know it's difficult to know he was nervous, but he was definitely acting edgy.

Eventually, she went into labour. Sky and I watched her give birth, and Leon, of course. The first one popped his head out - he was so cute! The next was a daughter. Then a third arrived, followed by the fourth, then then fifth. She had ten pups in all. Ten babies, all wanting their dinner at the same time. I looked at the father, he lay on the floor, just watching. He seemed very confused. I knelt beside him.

"Leon, you are a father now, life will be full of sleepless nights and crying babies." I started to laugh.

I found it hard looking at my shadow, the boy who has followed me everywhere, saving my life so many times. Now he was lying there, gazing at his missus and his ten pups. All the girls came to see the pups, they were born blind. It's hard to imagine how big they will eventually grow.

It was only a few weeks later when they started to eat meat. I hoped that they wouldn't eat as much as their father did, or all our rations would be gone in no time.

One day, I saw Leon dragging a deer into the palace courtyard. He had hunted to provide the food for his pups, rather than use our stores. I noticed two soldiers discussing the deer. One was suggesting to the other that it was wrong for all that fresh meat to be eaten by dogs, while they were eating salted beef if they were lucky. The second soldier agreed with him. The first one, now told the other to distract Leon, while the other dragged the deer away. Leon heard the soldiers eying his kill. He had now dropped the deer and was staring at the soldiers. Normally, no one can take his food from him. But this deer was for his pups. I am not sure if my whole army could have taken his deer from him. Leon started to growl; he was telling them that the deer was his. At the sight of Leon's teeth, the soldiers drew their swords. Well, it must have been these soldiers' lucky day, Sky had heard all the shouting, and she, like me, could see a problem. She managed to get behind these two soldiers. She then put her head between their heads, while putting one hand on each of the soldiers' heads. Then she stood back, and banged their heads together. What a woman.

I arranged the last meeting. Everyone was there on time. I had previously spoken with Quintin. I first asked him how he was getting on with the princess. His reply was what I had hoped for.

He explained that they had been together almost every day and that he cared for her a lot. He would miss her so much when the army departed. I also spoke with Shirin before the meeting, and I asked the same question about Quentin. She also replied that they had been together daily, and that she thought he was a wonderful man.

"Over the last few years, I have only been in the company of men, and these were men that I hated. Meeting Quintin was a breath of fresh air - I feel like I have been blessed. I will be heartbroken when he leaves with the army." She even asked if she could leave with us.

I stood at the end of the table. All eyes were on me, especially my wife's, as she knew what I was going to announce.

"Firstly, I will announce who will rule this empire after we have left." I now had their attention.

"The empress will be someone from the last ruling family," I paused for effect, then announced Princess Shirin as the empress. I looked at her - she looked disappointed. "I am also leaving someone who I have grown close to over the couple of years I have known him... Quintin, will you accept the role of Emperor? There is wealth and power in this position." Then added with a smile "The Empress is quite pretty as well." That got a laugh out of the room.

A smile lit up both Quintin and Princess Shirin's faces and they shared a caring look.

The meeting continued with agreements on sharing the wealth with the poor, a peace agreement between our empires, and other policies. After the meeting I explained to the pair that although they share power, I was not saying that they had to marry. That was for them to decide. They could simply share the roles, living separate lives if they pleased. The two of them looked at each other, and I knew that was not what would happen.

"I think I speak for both of us in saying that we have begun to fall in love," He looked at Princess Shirin, who gave him an encouraging look, then back to me.

"We want to marry. There are no Christian preachers in this city, so, commander, would you marry us before you leave?"

Now even I didn't expect that. As commander, I indeed had the power to marry them.

I rushed back to where we were staying, I could not wait to tell Sky how good a cupid I was. On entering the room, I fell over Leon. He was laying there, dreaming of his previous life before the children. Now, if Leon was a man, I would have taken him for a drink. But all I could do was to rub his belly - that always relaxes him.

CHAPTER EIGHT

LET'S TAKE MAE HOME

We were ready to depart. Quintin had provided us with supplies to keep us going for about three months. Princess Shirin gave me a wagon filled with gold and precious gems. I shared half the treasure between my soldiers.

I had lived in this city for about four months. Having entered the city as a conqueror, I now hoped that the people accepted me as a friend. When we were leaving Jerusalem, many people were telling me that the Sassanids were bad people, that they stole and killed.

I always remember what my father told me.

"Son, the people who cause wars, kill and leave misery in their wake, are not *the people*. People just follow orders. Kings, and others in power, order the actions which cause tears and death."

I was told how bad these people were, but now I have grown to love them. I left the city with a heavy heart. I hoped l would return one day."

One thing that did make me smile was the wagon. Well, two wagons. One wasn't big enough to hold ten growing pups. There was Beaue and five pups in one wagon; the other also had five pups, but Leon had been ordered by Beaue to stay in this wagon and look after them. I could see his face appearing out the back of the wagon, he was not into fatherhood. Of course, he loved his babies, but it was taking its toll on him. He needed to run across lush grassy fields, with the sun on his back. I would need to help him out at some point.

A few days before we were due to leave, several of my generals asked to meet me in private, I agreed of course, as I am always available to hear what my generals have to say. Although what they had to say on this occasion annoyed me. They queried as to why I plan to lead my army through two very big countries, in order to return Mae to her family. They informed me that my orders were to capture or kill the Sassanid emperor, and they believed that I should be taking the army back to Rome.

I asked the generals sternly, if they were now in charge of the Eastern Army. They realised that they may have overstepped the mark, and started to back off. I was now on the attack. I reminded them as to what Mae had done, to help us gain victories against the Sassanid. I also reminded them about how many Roman lives she had saved with her black powder. The generals now realised they were in trouble.

"Ok, if you wish to return to Rome, then I will comply with your wishes."

My generals were surprised with my answer. They all started to thank me. One, being braver than the others, asked if he should give the order for the army to prepare for their return to Rome. I asked him why he would do that.

"Well, you just told us that we can go back to Rome."

"That is correct," I replied. "You, and *just you,* can return to Rome."

"Sir," came the quick reply. "We can't travel all the way back to Rome on our own, we would be killed."

I turned my back on them, telling them as I walked away.

"That's up to you, go home, or come with us, your choice."

"Sir, that's not fair!" Shouted one of the generals. I turned and stormed back to face the loudmouth that was challenging me. Then I saw a familiar face near the door. Ok I will give you a chance, to have your way.

If all nine of you can kill my friend and me in a sword fight. You can lead the eastern army back to Rome.

They chatted amongst themselves, then suggested that someone should fight in my place, as I was the commander after all, and they didn't want to be seen as traitors.

"Can I replace myself with two women?" I suggested.

They had no problem with that. So, you have two women and a dog against all nine of us. If we kill them, we can lead the army back to Rome?

"Yes, that is what I am offering," I carped. "We are agreed. We will fight in two hours from now. Here!" I pointed to the spot that I was standing on.

I went to tell the lucky women about the fight, then returned to sit on my chair, ready to judge the result of the fight.

First the two women arrived, one was Sky, the other was Deana. The generals were waiting impatiently.

"Ok, so where is your dog?" the loudmouth asked. Into the room came Leon. Somehow, he had escaped from looking after his children and was here ready for some fun. It was nine against three.

The fight was over in ten minutes. Those generals would no longer be a problem.

"So, we are taking Mae home." I started standing up. "Let's go."

Just as I was about to order my army to leave, I had an idea. Deana had ten maids, Sky had four which she never used, and Lia also had four. I told the girls about Leon's problem. They all agreed to let me use their maids as puppy sitters.

"Onwards to India." I ordered.

And away my army marched. My army was well rested, well fed, and ready to go. We marched until sunset. The route I had chosen went west across Sassanid lands, into Northern India.

I had sorted the pup sitting by splitting the maids into two groups, then they were delegated into shifts. Leon was so happy, and even Beaue was pleased for the rest. The maids loved looking after the playful pups.

Where we camped was on the lower slopes of a mountain range. We were not far from a forest. I thought that some of my men would like to go hunting there.

Beaue let the pups play outside the wagon during the day. Of course, at night, they were returned to the wagons. That very evening, one of the maids fell asleep whilst on puppy watch. The pups in that wagon saw their chance to escape and have some moonlit fun and games. They quietly jumped out of the back of their wagon. Forests are dangerous places, particularly at night, and this night was no different. The pups were running around outside and underneath the wagon, oblivious to the fact they were being watched by three tigers.

Tigers are the largest of the big cats. In this case there was a mother with two hungry cubs to feed. These cubs were almost fully grown, nearly as big as their mother. Normally she would not dare hunt near a camp as big as ours, but hunger drives people, and animals, to do dangerous things. She had seen the pups playing with no humans around. She stalked them through the undergrowth, until she and her cubs were within sprinting distance.

Leon had a problem sleeping that night, so he decided to go for a walk around the camp. Perhaps this was fatherly instinct, or perhaps just luck, but either way this was extremely lucky for his cubs as he arrived just in time to face the tigers. Leon quickly positioned himself, in front of his cubs. To the tigress, this was a cat vs dog fight, and of course cats always win. The problem was that Leon was no ordinary dog, and these were his pups. Leon called for his pups to gather together behind him. The tigers began to circle them. The mother knew what she was doing, whereas her cubs were just copying her. Leon let out a very loud howl, to attract the attention of the rest of the camp. Beaue joined him in seconds. Now there were two parents protecting their young, against one parent trying to provide food for her young.

I wasn't far away, when I heard the Howl, I sprinted to Leon's aid as fast as I could, we have fought together many times. Soon we were joined by Sky, Deana, Lia, Mae and Kuuli, plus about thirty armed soldiers. The tigers were surrounded, the mother was worried for the safety of her cubs, while the cubs were starting to panic. I ordered everyone not to harm the tigers. This was just a mother trying to feed her babies after all. What mother would not want to feed her babies?

I ordered a few soldiers to go and fetch three lumps of meat. When they returned, I had the meat thrown to the tigers. I then ordered my soldiers to withdraw and create an opening for the animals to retreat with their meal into the forest. I then felt Sky's hand on my shoulder.

"Be careful my love, they may return tomorrow".

"Maybe. But we won't be here."

The following morning, the camp broke up early, and we were about an hour from moving on when I heard the sound of trumpets. I quickly ordered the soldiers to prepare for an attack. Then into view came Sassanid soldiers. There he was. General Shahpur.

The last time I saw him was before we took on the whole Sassanid army and conquered the capital. He dismounted and held out his hand.

"I bet you are surprised to see us again." I grabbed his offered hand and nodded in agreement with him.

"What are you doing here?" I asked

"You showed us mercy back in that valley. My men know that Rome and the Sassanid Empire are now friends. So, we wish to accompany you on your journey, until you return to our capital."

"Does your Empress know about this? I asked. "My new emperor, a man named Quintin, agreed for us to go with you. I believe you know him."

Good old Quintin, I thought.

"I will try to keep you and your men alive until you return to your country, I will make you and your twenty thousand men responsible for provisions and spare horses."

"Thank you, sir." came the generals reply.

"Tell your men that we leave in one hour."

We rode on for a few more days, Northern India had lots of very tall mountains. Two of my scouts charged up to me. They looked exhausted.

"Commander, we just witnessed a caravan of about thirty wagons, travelling this way."

"That's not a problem," I replied.

"No, the problem is there is a large army of Hun warriors approaching them," replied the scout.

"Huns? Why are Huns here? Bring all my light cavalry, and my foot soldiers who can now ride and fire arrows, to the front.

"Sorry Marcus, I need you and Anthony to take charge until we return."

We were too late. The caravan had been destroyed. There were bodies everywhere, most of the dead were civilians. I only saw a few Hun bodies. It was just a Slaughter. When a soldier fights another soldier, and one dies, that is war, which I am accustomed to. When four or five trained soldiers grab a helpless woman or kill innocent civilians, that makes me infuriated.

It didn't take us long to find where the Huns were camped. I had my men surround their camp, then ordered for their sentries to be killed.

At heart, I believe in mercy. But in some cases, like what I had just witnessed, I believe in punishment.

I had taken Deana, Mae, and Kuuli with me. Yes, Leon was with me, try and stop him going. We slowly edged ourselves down the slope towards their camp. They must have had a large army, because the camp fires lit up the skies for miles around. I ordered Deana and Mae to remain, while Kuuli and I slipped into the camp. I told Leon to shadow us. As it was a large camp, it took maybe forty-five minutes to reach where the prisoners were being held. What I saw was not pleasant. The Huns had a large fire burning and there were three men and two women, all tied to the ground. Eventually, after one of these men had been questioned and tortured. He was untied. I presumed that he was going to be moved elsewhere. Wrong. They lifted him up, then threw him into the fire. I was dumbfounded. I ordered Kuuli to return to Deana and Mae.

"Tell Mae to inform all my soldiers to attack the camp immediately. Then return to me with Deana. Our job will be to rescue the prisoners."

It wasn't long before Deana and Kuuli returned. I also knew that Leon was around somewhere. I don't need to give Leon orders; he can work out what he needs to do on his own.

The Huns continued to torture their prisoners. The next was a young woman. They started with the use of fire. I could not take any more. Mae had left six of her bags of black powder with me. I ordered Deana and Kuuli to keep together. Our job when the soldiers arrived, would be to all rush forward and protect the prisoners.

They were beginning to torture the older man. Lucky him, as my men arrived quickly. We rushed to the prisoners, turned and stood between them and the Huns. I killed two, then we were fighting back-to-back. Two Huns went to attack me from behind, but they met up personally with Leon.

"Hi Leon, I wondered where you were."

There were four of us defending three prisoners. Luckily, my soldiers did not take long to cover the ground to where we were. They came charging through the Huns. We were outnumbered but quick enough to take advantage of their surprise, collect all seven of us and get out of the camp.

Soon we were back with our main army. I ordered the medical

personnel to look after the three prisoners. Then I reported to Sky. I had to confirm that I was not hurt. Also, I needed to check that Leon had returned safely - he is a bit slower than the horses. It wasn't long before Leon returned.

"You had better go home mate, or your missus will be after you."

The short man among the prisoners wanted to speak with me as soon as possible. He informed me that the Huns had an army consisting of about a hundred thousand warriors who were heading this way.

"Why are they coming this way?" I asked.

"Because…" he then paused. "My name is Aaray. I am a close friend of a man named Chandragupta. My friend also has an army, but it's not as large as the Hun army. My friend is planning to create a new empire. The Gupta Empire. He plans to make this empire, one for the people. He wants to avoid wars and prevent the poor from starving. He has a dream of a golden period in India's history.

"That sounds good to me, it's a dream I can approve of." I confirmed.

"Please, could you use your army to support him?" pleaded Aaray.

I agreed to consider supporting this Chandragupta against the Huns, but first we had to disperse these Huns.

A scout rode up to me at great speed. The rider dismounted, and saluted.

"Sir, the scouts for the Huns have seen our army. They reported this to their leaders. It appears that they realise that they are on a hiding to nothing, against us."

"Will you cut to the chase soldier? What are they going to do now?"

"They have moved north to meet up with their main army."

On hearing this news, I ordered everyone to make camp. We needed to rest and plan our next move. What I didn't want to do was have a face-to-face battle with their army. I believed we would win, but the death toll on both sides would be high. My army would then be at a disadvantage in future battles, with a long journey still to travel.

I went back to my tent, and laid down on what we were using for a bed. Luckily Leon and Beaue sleep in the wagons now.

The door of my tent suddenly opened and a beautiful woman walked in. I immediately felt nervous. What did she want here? And if Sky catches me with her alone in our tent, would she believe the truth?

The woman was carrying a small silver tray, on this tray was a bottle of red wine, and a drinking vessel.

"Sir, this is a gift from the generals to congratulate you on rescuing the prisoners. Let me pour you a cup full, I understand this is a quality wine" advised the woman.

I was thirsty after the exertions of freeing the prisoners. So, I took the cup and drank the wine. It was very refreshing, and yes, I would say it was a quality wine. The woman put the tray on the floor beside me, bowed then left. I must have been very thirsty, as I poured another cup of wine. I was sitting on the edge of my makeshift bed, when my head started to spin. Then I developed a pain in my stomach. The pain grew stronger and eventually I passed out.

Sky entered the tent at some point to find me unconscious. She tried to wake me up, then shouted for help. Mae was the first to arrive. Sky asked Mae if she knew anything about herbs and medicine.

Mae told Sky to sit beside her.

"You are aware that I was kidnaped by Chinese pirates, then sold to an old Chinese man."

"I know that." acknowledged Sky.

"When the pirates brought me ashore, they were talking amongst each other, as to what they had planned to do with me. The old man was looking for shellfish behind some rocks, and heard what they had planned to do. As I have said before, the old man, who was to become my master, had a heart of gold. He approached the pirates and offered to buy me. They discussed the purchase price and made an agreement.

The one who appeared to be in charge of the pirates, told my future master to collect me in the morning. My master had already heard what they had planned to do with me that night. He bravely told the pirates that either I came with him now, or in the morning he would only pay half the price.

The pirates had a discussion, and reluctantly agreed for me to leave with my master that day. My master taught me how to speak four languages, how to make the black powder, and many other things. The reason I am telling you this is because he also taught me about herbs. If Beat has been poisoned, then I will need to find an antidote."

As Mae was telling this story she was tending to Beat.

First, Mae smelt the wine, then she checked Beat all over.

"The wine was most certainly poisoned. I believe I know the herb which is the antidote. It is a small yellow plant which grows in meadows near mountain streams."

"Then we begin the search for the flower now! I will take a thousand-foot soldiers with me," fumed Sky, obviously distraught at the fact her husband had just been poisoned.

"That would be foolish," advised Marcus as he walked into the room. "If you take a thousand-foot soldiers, and the Huns come across you, they will annihilate them. I suggest that Sky, Mae and Kuuli, dress as peasants and if any Huns come across you, tell them you are foraging for mushrooms or something."

"So that is why my husband left you in charge of the army. I will fetch them and do as you suggest."

As soon as they had left, Marcus called Deana, Lia and Anthony. He asked them to follow Sky, about ten minutes apart.

"And most importantly, don't let them see you."

Leon watched the two groups leave camp. He could tell that this was something to do with helping Beat, his best friend. He jumped off the wagon, without making a sound. Then moved into a trot, as he hoped to catch them before they got into any trouble.

Marcus gave orders to find the maid who brought the wine.

Sky was in a hurry to find this plant; she did not want her husband to die. The three of them were heading to a mountain stream. A local woman told them about a stream which flowed through and out from the side of this mountain, and winds across a meadow. The meadow, they were informed, was covered in bright, sweet-smelling flowers. It wasn't long before they arrived at the stream. All three stood and stared at the meadow, it was ablaze with colour.

"But which is the one with the antidote?" Cried Sky. "We could spend all day looking, while Beat dies!"

They decided to spread themselves out, by going to various areas of the meadow. The problem was that only Mae could identify the flower they were looking for. Mae told them to collect a handful of every small yellow flower they found.

Then what they dreaded, happened. Out of the corner forest, riding into the meadow, came maybe fifty Huns. Kuuli reacted first, he told Sky and Mae to hide in the long grass. Kuuli then put his hands in the air.

Their leader, through an interpreter, asked why Kuuli was here and not working. Kuuli responded by telling them that he did not feel well this morning, so he took the day off work, and came here to do some fishing.

"Are you trying to catch your dinner?" the Hun leader pondered. Then he started to laugh. "How will you catch your dinner without a rod?"

"I usually dive in the water and catch the fish with my hands."

The Hun leader slapped Kuuli around the face. Kuuli was infuriated, and went for his dagger. Twenty swords pointing at him, made him return to normal. He fell to his knees and begged the Hun to forgive him, he told the leader that he had an anger problem, and that he was sorry.

"Are you good at fishing?" he asked. "Actually, don't bother to answer that. What I really want to know is, are you good with that dagger of yours?"

"Not particularly sir, I only really use my knife to clean the fish I catch."

The Hun made a gesture to his men. They fell back and created the shape of a large ring. You will fight me now, Mr Fisherman. You have your knife. Use it.

The two men stood in the centre of the ring, facing each other. Then Kuuli fell to the floor with an arrow sticking out of his right calf.

"I am so sorry, one of my archers fired his arrow by mistake." Two Huns lifted Kuuli up. "Are you ready now Mr Fisherman?"

Deana, Anthony and Lia had arrived and were waiting between the trees. Mae and Sky were not far away. The problem was that neither of them could help Kuuli.

The Hun made several lunges, but Kuuli was too fast for him, and swiftly avoided them. The Hun knew that Kuuli was losing blood and would tire as the fight went on.

Two women with a lot to lose were hiding not far away from the fight, but they were helpless.

Leon had arrived some time ago, and was waiting for a chance to do his thing. He moved among the crowd, without any attention being raised. Eventually he was on the edge of the ring. Kuuli had fought well but the loss of blood was taking its toll. Finally, he fell, the Hun stood above him ready to make the kill. As he lifted his sword ready to end Kuuli's life. Leon rushed out of the crowd and leapt on the now helpless Hun. Soon after, Deana, Lia and Anthony joined in the fight, followed by Sky and Mae.

"It is a nice day to die," declared Deana.

Sky looked at her, perplexed, and wondered if she was giving up. Deana smiled.

"Don't worry, I am talking about these Huns dying, not us."

There were six of the best fighters, plus Leon, the best of them, against fifty Huns, armed to the teeth. There is a saying that quality is better than quantity. Soon, about thirty of the enemy were dead and the rest were fleeing for the trees.

"At least we survived that little episode, but we haven't found the flower. Time is running out to save Beat," said Sky with a tear in her eye. "We must continue our search.

"You, Sky, need a little more faith" with that, Mae held out her hand. In her palm was a small yellow flower, apparently the one they had been searching for.

They all rushed back to their horses, Deana was helping Kuuli, as the arrow caused him to limp and the fight had taken all his energy. Leon started back as soon as he saw the yellow flower. He needed a headstart against the horses, and he was anxious to see Beat.

CHAPTER NINE

CHANDRAGUPTA

T he six of them returned as fast as they could. My life was depending on how quickly the antidote was given to me. Finally, Mae had the antidote prepared. She boiled the petals of the flower, then Sky gently spooned the liquid into my mouth.

In two days, the fever left me, but it took a week before I was able to walk. Marcus was the man I always thought he was. He was running the army as good as I would have, in fact (don't tell him), maybe he was slightly better. I guess with all that training he had, he should be better than me.

The main thing that Marcus was concentrating on was tracking down the general, or generals who had sent the poisoned wine. When he came to my bedside and informed me that he had located the generals responsible, I was shocked at how quickly he had found them.

"Do you remember the Generals who wanted you to take the army back to Rome?"

"Yes, of course I do, where are they now?", I demanded.

"They are in the next room waiting for your judgement, sir."

I had not fully recovered, but with the support of Marcus and Sky, I managed to get to a seat. There they were, five people who have spent their lives in luxury, always ordering people about to serve them. If they had killed me, I believe that Marcus would have taken control of the Army, but the five Legions which these generals commanded would have left and returned to Rome, causing problems.

They were all kneeling before me, begging for their lives. After all, killing, or even plotting to kill your commander, is treason. I managed to stand.

"I have heard you plead for your lives, I have listened, and decided that no one in this camp will be allowed to kill you." I watched them thanking me, bowing their heads. "Although no one here will kill you. I have decided that you all can go home to Rome. General Marcus, I order you to have these men stripped of their ranks, then provided with food and water for seven days, give them a horse each. Then have them driven out of the camp and order the army to kill them if they ever return!"

One morning, Leon came up to me. I asked him how he was doing. His response was to grab my arm in his mouth and pull me. Negotiation has never been part of Leon's skills, he makes a decision, and I have to fall in with it. As it was, this time I was pleased to have gone with him. There was Beaue with her ten pups. They took me back to when Leon was a pup. That bundle of fluff. Here we had ten bundles of fluff. I sat on the ground stroking Beaue. Your pups are growing fast young lady, I praised her for their good parenting skills. Soon I was lying flat on the ground with ten pups jumping all over me.

"Do you need any help?" asked Sky with a smile on her face.

She was soon in the middle having a rough and tumble (with the pups of course).

I was feeling a lot better after a week and decided to return to my duties. My first job was to arrange a meeting with Aaray and talk about this Chandragupta.

We met up in the early evening. It was cool and the stars were twinkling, I tried counting them, but I soon gave up. Aaray arrived a little late, but it wasn't a problem.

Chandragupta was king of the Gupta Dynasty. He had been crowned early that year. His marriage to Princess Kumara Devi, was about to take place.

"He has an army," explained Aaray, "But compared to the Huns, his army is small. I have heard that the Huns are moving at speed towards their capital, the city of Pataliputra (modern day Patna), which lies at the confluence of two rivers - the Son and the Ganges. If the Huns destroyed his army, they would fall upon the Indian people, they would slaughter the old and the young. You are the voice of Rome; will you send your army to help us? King Chandragupta is on his way to meet you. He is travelling in secret as if his enemies were aware of this, they would try to capture him."

I asked Aaray, as to which route his king would be coming. He replied that he planned to meet him on the way. He planned to leave immediately, so I asked Deana, Kuuli and Anthony to take a hundred of our heavy cavalrymen and escort the king.

"Are you sure, my love, that you should not meet the king and escort him yourself?"

"You are right, Sky. I should go with them and leave Marcus in charge."

"That is a good decision. I will go and change for the journey." She had done it again, with a few sweet words, she had gotten herself included in the escort party. I walked away, mumbling to myself that I may as well ask her to just tell me if she *doesn't* want to be included in something. It would be so much quicker.

An hour later we were on our way. I was excited to meet this man. I had heard a lot about him. Sky wasn't far behind me, and Leon had also decided to come along. I presume he needed a break from the kids.

Sky had ordered ten of her warriors to find the Huns, and bring up to date details. With all the things going on I had all but forgotten the Huns, lucky Sky always had my back.

The weather was hot and sultry, we were travelling through a forest - or should I call it a jungle? I could hear the sounds of various birds, with the occasional roar of large mammals. The sounds of the big cities were now far behind. I had ordered the rest of my army to follow about two hours behind.

Eventually we left the forest, and proceeded onto a stony path. I had got used to the sounds, which we had just left behind, but nothing prepared me for what I was about to encounter. I heard what could only be described as loud trumpeting. Then into view came a huge animal. I had never seen anything like it before. I could see a man sitting on its back carrying a spear. I ordered my company to halt. I was unsure what I should do next. Aaray rode alongside my horse. Have no fear my friend, this is a war Elephant. In battle, the elephants charge forward and trample the enemy. Also, they create so much fear with the enemy soldiers, and their horses. King Chandragupta will be riding on the third Elephant. I suggested that we make camp and prepare a meal for the king.

It took nearly an hour to prepare the meal. Aaray told me that he would ride to meet the king and prepare him for our meal and meeting.

The king arrived and I made him welcome. Aaray carried out the translation as I did not have anyone who could speak the language of King Chandragupta.

As we ate, I often saw signs on the King's face telling me he wasn't enjoying the meal. Aaray kept telling me that the king was enjoying the meal. I asked Sky what her thoughts were.

"He doesn't like the food. In India, food is always hot and spicy. Roman food to him is bland" That wasn't Sky's voice. I turned and there was Mae, with a big smile on her face.

"And how do you know what he is saying?" I asked her. Mae told me that on her way from China, she had to cross parts of India, where she picked up some of the language.

"It was lucky that she followed you, my love."

"Very true Sky, and thank you Mae, for using your initiative, and intelligence, unlike I did." She was very graceful and forgiving. She told me that I had the responsibilities of the whole army. I can't be expected to remember everything. If I only manage to carry out just one more thing before I die, I will get Mae back to her family.

Later, I had a one-to-one chat with Chandragupta. He came across to me as a nice man, but also very intelligent. But far more than this, he had a heart for his people.

Finally, I agreed to use my army to keep the Huns away from his capital, and to protect him and the princess. His response was to offer me use of his war Elephants. He promised to provide one hundred war Elephants, and ended our meeting by offering us a ride on one of his Elephants.

Standing beside these majestic beasts, could only be described as awesome. They ooze so much power. I closed my eyes and imagined them charging an enemy, trampling them under foot.

Ok, who is going to ride this one with you? Came the question from his mahout. My reply was easy, I smiled as I gave the name.

"Sky, of course! Then the next pair will be Deana and Kuuli, then Marcus and Lia, next Mae will share her Elephant with Antony."

My Elephant knelt down. I had to stand on one of his legs, but somehow, I managed to climb from his knee to get on his back. Looking down, it was high enough already. Then the Elephant stood up. 'Help! I am going to fall off and die', I thought. Finally, it came to me. I was looking across the people below, and was feeling oh so powerful. I was in control. I could throw spears and fire arrows, but no one could reach me. Then I nearly had a heart attack as the Elephant decided to lay down again. I had forgotten that he had to pick up Sky as well.

After we had all experienced riding an Elephant, I gave the signal for us to get off. The mahout decided to play a game with us. A trunk suddenly appeared and wrapped itself around my waist. I was lifted off the Elephant, as if I was a feather, carried through the air and gently lowered to the ground. Sky was looking down and laughing so hard that I thought she was going to fall off. Then the trunk that had made her laugh so much, wrapped itself around her, and it lifted her into the air with ease. My warrior woman was now screaming and I was the one splitting my sides with laughter. Then I saw that she had stopped screaming and was staring down at me. I quickly took the smile off my face. Then she started to laugh, she could see the funny side, but was glad to get her feet back on the ground. As she landed, I was there and we shared a hug. My new friend Chandragupta, tapped me on my shoulder.

"Will a hundred of my pets be of help to you he asked?" I put my arm around his shoulder.

"They could be very helpful." I replied

"I will also supply archers to ride them. My friend, I think the Huns are in for a big surprise."

Magnus and Lia, were sitting on a rock chatting, Marcus was apologising for not being able to see Lia lately. Marcus, I understand, my parents were senators, I know how much work is involved in positions of authority.

"Lia, I think I have fallen in love with you. He said, staring lovingly into her eyes. "If I am out of place, please forgive me".

Lia stared back at him.

"When I first met you, I thought you were a good man, and I could see there was a lot more to you. During these months we have spent together, I have felt close to you. I have been hurt in the past, and I am cautious of men," she paused momentarily. "But I now feel a place in my heart for you. Let's see how close we become, before I can accept your love fully."

Kuuli and Deana, were sparring in a nearby field. They were both skilled at martial arts. Who was the best, I don't know? One day one would win, another day, the other would triumph. Today I was passing, and decided to watch for a bit. One thing was for sure, they didn't take it easy. They would ache tomorrow, I thought. Then Kuuli tossed Deana over his shoulder, and she landed on her back. Kuuli was concerned that she may be hurt, he fell to his knees beside her, as she lay motionless. He put his hands on her shoulders, that was what she was waiting for, in one movement, Kuuli was on his back with Deana on top of him. I heard him say that he had fallen for her.

Deana leant forward and kissed him. I started to blush, time for me to go. I shot off to find Aaray.

The scouts had returned. The Huns had an army of about one hundred and thirty thousand warriors. They were all on horseback and experts at using their bows as they rode. They were heading towards the capital city of Pataliputra and had just left the city of Ayodhya.

"Chandragupta, is there a valley on the way to Pataliputra?" I asked.

"I do know one, about twenty miles from my Capital. Steep hills on either side with lots of trees growing on the hillside. The valley is about three miles across."

I told him that would be ideal. He then asked me if I was going to send my whole army against them. He reminded me that I had the majority of the soldiers. I asked him to sit beside me.

"My friend, when I was given my first command, I promised that I would always give my men a chance to survive. I promised to always do my best to bring all my soldier's home, after any campaign. My promise has never changed, no matter how big my advantage in numbers is, I still aim to help all my men to survive. Just get your Elephants to the valley, and I will show you how to win a battle, and avoid the mass slaughter of your troops. Just leave me some scouts to direct my army to that valley, and I will meet you and your Elephants there in three days."

Chandragupta and his entourage left soon after our chat. I ordered

Marcus to organise our departure, then I searched for Lia. I found her alone in her tent.

"Hi Lia, long time no see." She looked at me and smiled.

"I am only alone now because you have given Marcus orders. You did that on purpose." I smiled back and replied that I did want to speak with her alone.

"Lia, we are on our way to fight a big battle, we will win, but, in a head-to-head, man-to-man encounter, many men on both sides will die. I made a promise to always give my men a chance to survive, to live." I paused before I spoke again, I needed to compose myself. "Lia, there have been many times since I watched your sister dying, when I have prayed to God for help. I don't know why, as I have never told him that I accepted him. But in three days' time, I will need him to protect my men again.

"Beat, my friend, you once told me that as you watched my sister burn, that you could not understand how she accepted her death without any fear. You also said that she looked as if someone was protecting her from the flames. I believe that you know who was with her in her pain." She held my hands. "Jesus has always been with you; he is just waiting for you to accept him. Let us pray together for the protection of your troops."

We prayed, and it's funny, but as I left her tent, I felt so much confidence that my men would be safe.

I agreed to meet Chandragupta in three days, and we arrived in exactly three days. I sat on my horse looking at the Elephants. They looked awesome standing together in such a large, powerful herd. My plan was the same as I have used before, with a small twist. I had been informed that the Huns were still one day behind us.

I ordered trees to be cut down, and rolled into the valley. The Elephants with their great strength, lifted the trunks and piled them up along either side. They were also piled at the end of the valley.

Only one thing was needed now - a way to pull the Huns into the valley. Any good leader would avoid sending his men into a valley such as this. It clearly looked like a trap.

There is only one reason they would charge into this valley.

"Are you talking to yourself again my love?"

"Sky, I am going to get myself caught by the Huns. Somehow you have to get me freed, then as we escape, join with fifty thousand of our troops and charge into this valley."

"You want me to creep into a camp with about one hundred and thirty warriors camped there?" I nodded my head.

"I plan to get captured as soon as they arrive tomorrow. So have your plan prepared."

I then went off to see Leon. There he was, lying on the ground surrounded by his pups.

"Leon, I don't think you'd be interested, but I need someone to risk his life to save me."

I have known Leon for many years but this was the fastest that he reacted to any of my requests. I looked at their pups,

"Wow, they are growing so fast!"

By the time the moon had set, a plan was ready. I was going to pretend to be a spy and get caught. Sky and the others were going to rescue me. Then we would rush to the entrance of the valley and be joined by fifty thousand of my troops. We would all then charge into the valley. The Huns would charge into the valley in pursuit, knowing that there is an exit, and hoping to catch us. It would all depend on Sky rescuing me, but I had a plan B, just in case. Leon would be coming!

I rode up to the edge of their camp, then left my horse and crept along the ground towards the nearest tent. It took longer than I thought for their guards to capture me. I was dragged before their leader. He slapped me a few times before asking me what I was doing there. I explained that I and others were assessing his strength. He ordered his men to interrogate me. I was dragged away to another tent and as they were about to start the torture, I admitted that I was Beat, the commander of the Eastern Roman army. The interrogator rushed off to tell the leader. This was it. Either I was rescued now, or it could be a painful night. Ten minutes later, there was no sign of Sky. I was starting to think my plan had failed, and the result would be seen in the blood of my men.

I was glad I had arranged for a plan B. There he was the daddy, and still my boy, it was Leon. He removed the guards and then freed me from my bond quickly. The two of us rushed out of the tent and ran as fast as we could to where the horses were tied. As I arrived, there were Sky, Deana, Lia, Mae, and Kuuli, my rescue party. They had decided it would be best to send in my seasoned rescuer. By now we could hear noise everywhere.

"Ok, let's move," we galloped at top speed.

As we approached the valley, we could see our cavalry waiting. Although we rode fast, we made sure we kept the Huns in sight, we needed them to catch us meeting the cavalry, as we rode into the valley. Our pursuers stopped and we could see they had sent messengers back to report to their leader. This was it, either they brought all their army to chase us into the valley. Or they hold back and we would have to fight it out man to man on the plains. For a while I sat and prayed. Then there it was, the whole of their army charging towards us.

We all charged into the valley. I jumped off my horse after entering, as I needed to climb up the nearest hill to be able to direct the battle. The rest of the riders rode to the end of the valley, dismounted and hid behind the wall of tree trunks. The Huns charged into the valley. They smelt victory. However, ten minutes' ride into the valley, thousands of arrows fell into their warriors. My men on the hillside and hidden behind tree trunks at the side of the road all had bows. The bodies of Hun warriors lay all over the floor of the valley. Their leader sounded retreat and what was left of their army turned and charged back the way they had come. Then the Elephants entered the valley. One hundred war Elephants, I doubt if the Huns had ever seen an Elephant. They had metal plates in different places to protect them from arrows and the mahouts all had bows or spears. Ready to bring more death on the hapless Huns. I ordered the Elephants forward; the Huns were panicking. I then waved a white flag from where I was high up on one side of this hill. The leader of the Huns also raised a white flag. I came down the hill, and fifty of my Soldiers who were behind the tree trunks at the side of the valley, came out and marched behind me. I introduced myself as Commander Zug of the Eastern Roman army. He also held out his hand and introduced himself as Bleda. I pointed out that my men had arrows pointed at all or at least most of his warriors, and I had a hundred war Elephants waiting to charge his remaining men.

As always, I don't like killing people for the sake of it. I offered Bleda the chance to lay down their weapons, then collect their dead and wounded, and go back to where they come from. Bleda was not a fool, and gratefully accepted my offer. As he left with his warriors, he looked into my eyes and made a statement, 'We will meet again someday', and off he rode.

If only I could have read the future, I would have realised what a mistake I had just made.

CHAPTER TEN

THE LAND OF THE DRAGON

Chandragupta, invited us all to his palace for dinner. It was only open to generals and above of course, no room for the bulk of my army, they ate outside. There were some interesting dishes. One dish was sheep's eyes. I got the impression that they ate *every* part of the animal. The last dish smelled wonderful and I had avoided eating many of the dishes, but this dish smelt so nice I could not wait to eat it. There it was, finally sitting on a dish in front of me, asking me to eat it. I picked up my spoon, filled the spoon to the top with this delicious dish.

"Help me!" I whimpered as I tried to remove every bit of the food from my mouth.

I drank a whole bottle of wine to try and ease the pain. My mouth was burnt. In some parts of my mouth there were blisters. I had never tasted anything so hot.

Sky and I left the palace early, it had been a hard day and I needed to sleep.

"Hi their young man."

It was Leon, having a break from the pups. After giving him a big hug, I noticed something move in the trees. Before I could react, Sky's body was in front of me. She looked into my eyes, then collapsed. I held her tight, supporting her, then I saw an arrow sticking in her back. I dropped to my knees and laid Sky on her side. She was now unconscious. I could not stop crying.

"Someone! Help me! Please!" I sobbed and pleaded.

Mae ordered two soldiers to carry Sky to a nearby tent.

"Don't touch her! I will carry my wife."

I carried her into the tent still crying. Mae told me to leave Sky to her.

"Please save her," I cried.

Mae gave me a hug, then told me to leave. She promised to save her.

While I was taking care of Sky, Leon had seen the assassin. Leon being Leon, was across the ground and into the trees in a second. A few minutes later he was dragging this young woman towards my tent. As I arrived back with Lia and the others, I saw Leon with this young woman and red mist suddenly came over me. I drew my sword out of its scabbard. I was almost to her, when Leon stood in front of her. Move over boy, she may have killed my wife, it's payback time. Leon stood his ground, he knew that the monster wearing my uniform was not the man he had grown up with. I wasn't sure how I was going to get past him. Leon was stronger than me, faster than me, and in fact all round superior.

Then Beaue came and stood next to the young woman. Now I have no chance of getting to the woman without someone getting hurt. Then the winning move. Ten very large pups came and surrounded the young woman. My rage had gone, I was laughing so hard I was crying.

"Ok, I got the message." Then I gave Leon a big hug. That was a mistake as ten pups, followed by their mother all jumped on me. Still lying on the ground, I ordered Antony to put the young woman in my tent with ten guards.

"Do you want me to interrogate her sir?"

'Interrogate' is Roman for torturing someone until they admit what you want them to say.

"No! Give her food and wine, I will be back in an hour." I then rushed over to see if Sky had survived.

That wife of mine is made of rock. I had left her, unconscious, with an arrow in her back. Now she was sitting up and laughing with Mae. As I entered the tent, Mae told me that the arrow had been removed, and the wound had stopped bleeding. I walked over to Sky and kissed her passionately.

"Thank you for saving my life, my love." She looked at me then said

"If I hadn't, who would I have to beat up?" Then she laughed, wincing a little as it caused pain where her wound was.

"Mae said you will have to stay in bed for about seven days." She then made a face as though she was going to cry.

"I can't stay in bed for seven days, please let me out early my love!"

"Ok, three days then. Darling, don't you want me to warm you in bed? Last offer, two days here."

"Ok," she replied and laid down. That was good… I didn't think she would stay in bed at all.

I sat in my tent waiting for the young woman to be brought in. I had been wondering why a young woman would want to kill me. I had never seen her before. Ten minutes later, she was standing before me.

"How old are you?" I asked

"Eighteen," she replied, "I suppose you will be interrogating me now. It's ok. I am not afraid to die."

I ordered a soldier to bring her a chair. Then I poured her a goblet of wine.

"As far as I know, I have never met you before, so why do you want to kill me?"

"You killed my father." was her reply. I could see the hatred in her eyes towards me.

"And who was your father?" I asked. "My father was one of the five generals who you drove out of the camp. I am sure that by now he must be dead."

I sat in silence, before I responded. I explained everything that happened. Finalising with the poisoned wine.

"Tell me, what would you have done with them?"

I reminded her that trying to kill your commander was treason, punishable by death. She was silent for a while; I was wondering what she was thinking.

"Needlessly you sent them out into a foreign land, where they will have enemies everywhere. You are responsible for the death of my father, and I *will* kill you for it." At that point Sky entered the tent. She was very annoyed.

"Your father committed treason! He poisoned the commander of the Eastern Roman army. Then, you also committed treason by trying to kill him also. Sky walked up to the young woman and pointed her knife at her neck.

"You tell us how the commander should punish you for trying to kill him". The woman hung her head, and was silent for a while. Then she lifted her head defiantly.

"Kill me however you want, without my father, I have no will to live". Sky was now getting angry.

"You are quick to judge, let me tell you something. Your father poisoned my husband. Yes, he had the generals driven out of the camp. It would have been fitting if they had all been killed by the first band of thieves that they met. But no, my husband who you were so willing to kill, sent a hundred soldiers to watch over them, to give the same men who tried to kill him, protection. They have prevented ten attacks so far, and all the traitorous generals are still alive. The soldiers are under orders to follow the generals all the way back to Rome. This is the man who you tried to kill."

What a woman, she should be in the senate making speeches like that.

Finally, the young woman broke down, she fell to her knees and begged for forgiveness. Lia, who had been watching the proceedings in silence, decided to speak.

"I have known this young woman for several years. Back in Rome our families were friends. Her name is Acilla, she has always been a kind and helpful girl, well a woman now. Beat, I mean commander, I beg you to show her mercy."

"Lia, I never had any intention to harm her. I just want her to understand that she was wrong to judge me before doing any research. But I am glad that you have come forward and spoke on her behalf. Lia, will you accept becoming her guardian?" Lia nodded.

"Acilla, will you accept Lia as your guardian?". She nodded as well. Thank God, they both agreed. There I go again, thanking God. One thing was for sure, God was playing an important part in my life. I returned to Chandragupta, to say my farewell.

"My friend, I thank you for our provisions. Be a great leader for your people, love them, and care for them."

I waved a sad farewell; we could have been great friends. He had given me ten scouts who spoke mandarin and were familiar with our route.

We travelled through three smaller countries before we entered the

'Land of the Dragon'. The scouts informed me that we had entered an area of China ruled by the Eastern Jin. They told me that the Eastern Jin Dynasty was ruled by Emperor Yuan. They also offered to inform me about the history of the Eastern Jin Dynasty. As information is the main ingredient for success, I grabbed the chance they were offering.

In 311 AD, the Jin Dynasty was overrun by the Northern tribal peoples and the North of China was lost.

The invasion of nomads in the North prompted droves of people to emigrate south of the Yangtze River.

Upon hearing about the fall of Chang'an, Sima Rui founded the Eastern Jin Dynasty in 317 AD. The Eastern Jin had limited power. They were dependent on noble families, who had emigrated. The capital of the Eastern Jin, was the city of Jian Kang. The city lay on the south coast of China, meaning it would be a great place to find ships to take Mae home. I thanked the scouts for the valuable information and asked them to lead my army across this land, until we reached this city.

As we travelled, it was clear to see the diversity of this country. Peasants up to their knees in water, planting rice. We came across many poor people trying to scrape together a living. At times like this I appreciated the life I had. A beautiful wife, lots of friends, and the best friend anyone could ever have, my Leon. At that point I was woken from my daydreams. Leon had arrived, but he wasn't alone. I had to smile; he had his pups with him. They were almost full grown. I was thinking about our time back home. Leon, myself and the other ten members of his pack. Now he had made his own pack. I halted my horse and jumped off. Come here Leon, I have missed you. I threw my arms around him. A big mistake. If anyone hugs the dad, it becomes a family thing, I was now part of the Leon and Beaue family. Yes, you have got it. Ten, now massive, pups all jumped on me at once. Leon tried to rescue me, but even he had no chance. Twenty minutes later I managed to crawl out from under the pack. Beaue, gave me a motherly licking. I somehow got back on my horse, then looked at Leon. Take care of them. You are now the commander of my special team. Take your team to where the meat is kept and tell them I ordered him to provide special snacks today. I had arranged beforehand that when Leon turned up with his family, that they would each be given some meat, preferably on a bone. Leon was off, with his pups running along behind.

Then Sky rode up alongside

"Are you ok to ride a horse? Shouldn't you be riding in a wagon?" I asked. She still hadn't completely recovered from the arrow. She looked at me and smiled

"I can outride you anytime." And she could.

I saw the poor, but as we travelled, I also had the pleasure of seeing the countryside, and birds I had never seen before.

Just as the sun was beginning to set, we were approaching a small village. People were running everywhere in a panic. Then I saw the reason for their distress. The village was being attacked by barbarians. I had never seen them before but they would regret ever seeing me. I ordered Marcus to surround the village with the heavy cavalry. I called Leon and his special team forward, then called Deana, Kuuli, Mae, and fifty of my foot soldiers (I thought they may like a chance to walk rather than ride). I led this group forward at the same time the heavy cavalry moved forward. My group split into teams. Leon had his own team and there were ten soldiers each for Kuuli, Deana, and Mae.

"Ten for you. That leaves ten for me my love, I know you would not forget me." I asked her if she was fit enough for this, but of course she told me that she was.

"Ok, our teams will go in together. That's five teams."

My team rode through the middle of the village. We had been waiting for some action since crossing the border. Also, I couldn't stand injustice.

We had soon killed or captured all the Barbarians. Well, at least I thought we had, but then came screams from one of the buildings. Sky, Deana, and I rushed over to the building. As we arrived, maybe five of these savages came out with a young woman held hostage. The one who appeared to be their leader had a knife to her throat. Mae came to my side, as a translator, but she knew nothing about this language. Then along the road came Leon and his team - the special team. I ordered everyone to sit down. We'd leave it to the special team.

Leon and his team were behind the hostage situation. He signalled his pups to lay down and be silent. Then He and Beaue crept along the ground, inching slowly towards the man with the knife. The man who I had presumed to be the leader was becoming agitated by the fact that we were all just sitting on the ground and ignoring him. Then he finally began to speak.

"I want seven horses brought here. Then all your men must disarm. I am taking this woman with me and if anyone attempts to rescue her, she will die."

A couple of his warriors looked around the area.

"They have no soldiers near us sir, only a pack of dogs."

"Why are you telling me about Dogs? What harm will they do?"

I heard his statement. I could have given him the answer, but it was more interesting to watch Leon and his team in action. Leon and Beaue crept closer and closer to the woman. Then with a short sprint, Leon was on the man with the knife in seconds. Leon went for the knife hand whilst Beaue knocked the woman over and stood in front of her, providing her with protection. The remaining barbarians turned to face Leon. Their leader was now unconscious. It was now Leon against five of the savages. Now I know Leon would have no problem dispatching them, but he had to train his team. He made a low growl and immediately the pups gathered around the enemy. It was amazing, they all laid down on the ground awaiting Leon's orders. Leon had no intention for his pups to be harmed - he and Beaue attacked first.

There was panic among the barbarians. While Leon was dealing with two of them, another raised his sword ready to strike. I drew my sword and ran towards him, but before I got anywhere near, one of Leon's pups leapt upon him. Just like Leon, he grabbed the man by his throat, The warrior dropped to the ground, unconscious. This encouraged the rest of the Pups, who now all attacked. The encounter was soon over. It was the first battle for my special team, which of course resulted in victory. I could never beat Leon at wrestling, now with ten pups as well, I have less than no chance.

Now it was interrogation time. The first thing I needed to know was, who were they? This didn't take long as one of the villagers soon came up and told me. They were Tartars. They had come from the North; they broke through the Great Wall, then destroyed the Northern Jin, before crippling the Western Jin. Now they were moving south.

I turned to their leader and asked him how many Tartar warriors there were? He told me everything, he wasn't scared.

"We have over 500,000 warriors. They will crush the Eastern Jin and rule over the whole of China."

What to do with them? I set them free. They could return to their leaders and inform them as to whom they were up against. I had the guards drive them out, then I gathered my leaders. Our target was still the same, to get to the capital of the Eastern Jin Empire, Jian Kang. My scouts informed me that we were about half way across the Jin Empire.

We were not far from a small city called Changsha. I figured it would be best to stop there for a chance to refuel before we made our final journey to the Capital and met up with Emperor Yuan.

What I hadn't known when I decided to stop there, was that the emperor was staying in Changsha. We arrived late in the day. I sent Lia with Marcus and a hundred of my soldiers into the city. They were met by the emperors' representatives, and made welcome. The emperor agreed to meet up with me in the morning. At last! A good night's sleep.

The following morning, I was woken up by Sky punching me on my back.

"What's the matter Sky? Let me sleep a little more."

"If I slept like you, my love, you would be dead."

Now that did rouse me. I jumped out of the bed and tripped over a body. What a wife! I was lying flat on the floor next to a corpse and all she could do was laugh. It turned out that a Tartar warrior had entered our tent last night. Luckily Sky was awake, and that was the end of him. We dressed quickly, and made ourselves smart to meet the emperor. There were eight of us who would be meeting the emperor.

I had heard before that these Emperors threw massive celebrations. Petals were scattered across the floor, then we were all taken to separate rooms. He was making us welcome in a big way. Sky was brought with me. First, we were both undressed by these naked women, then led to a massive bath. There we were both washed and covered in sweet smelling perfumes. I won't tell you what Sky was saying to me - I could not print what she said. Then we were both dressed in Chinese garments.

"I bet you want to hug me now. I smell amazing!" I said turning to Sky.

If looks could kill, I would be dead now.

"Hug you? That is the last thing I want to do with you." She whispered. "I understand that what just happened is customary, and you had to just go along with it, but at least you could pretend you did not enjoy it so much."

She then smiled and threw her arms around me. When I met Sky, I won the Jackpot.

Then a thought occurred to me. I had brought Leon with me, I wondered where he was. I started to look in different bathrooms (luckily *most* were empty). Then I opened one door and there he was. He was standing on the side of the bath looking very sorry for himself. Sky had also arrived and the two of us stood there laughing. Leon looked at us, then sprinted over and jumped on both of us, he soaked us both. He was not finished yet, yes, he pushed us both in his bath. We had to get dried and dressed all over again. There it was again. I swear that Leon can laugh.

Eventually we all arrived in the emperor's banqueting hall. It was an amazing celebration. Then it came to the important part. The emperor said that he had heard about our exploits in India, and was hoping that I would send my army, or to be more exact, the Eastern Roman army.

I first asked him how many soldiers he had to fight the Tartars. His response was 100,000 soldiers. But they would have to defend his capital, so he could instead offer to order 300,000 peasants to join us.

I stood to my tallest height, and informed him that my orders are to return to Rome as soon as possible. Therefore, I was unable to order my soldiers to fight the Tartars. Suddenly, the Emperor stood up in front of his throne. He approached me then started to speak.

"Roman, if the Tartars reach the town of Badong before the villagers can escape, they will all be slaughtered. Will you be able to sleep, with all these deaths on your conscience?"

I stood and scratched my head for a while. Then I turned and spoke with the emperor.

"You are right. I cannot leave those villagers to the mercy of the Tartars. I will lead a force there now to try and rescue them. We will not try to fight the Tartars, just support the villagers in their attempt to flee."

I ordered all my light cavalry to be ready in one hour. I decided to take Sky, Mae, and Deana with me. Lia called across to me and asked me to talk with Acilla before we left. I rushed over and caught her.

"I understand that you wish to speak with me."

She told me that she had been trained to fight and begged me to let her go with them. Eventually I agreed. As soon as we were all ready we left, heading north.

CHAPTER ELEVEN

ESCAPE FROM BADONG

I took with me twenty thousand light cavalry. These men carried a sword and a bow. They travelled light and their horses seemed to eat up the miles as we raced to beat the Tartars to the town of Badong.

We arrived before the Tartars, but had no idea of how long it would be before they arrived. This reminded me of the time some years ago, when I was relieving a town in Northern Italy. That time the Goths were following us. I had to order the burning of all their crops as I could not leave food for the Goth army. I had no choice but to order the same here. Five hundred of my soldiers rode around the fields, burning everything. The funny thing was that the town's own troops turned out and tried to stop my men from carrying out my orders.

The rest of my command rode into the town. There were people running everywhere, with no organisation at all. I sent a squad into their council building. Ten minutes later, a group of citizens were driven out. I dismounted and introduced myself. They showed little interest and went back to collecting as many valuables as they could carry. I told the guards to leave them, our priority was to rescue the people. I gathered the townspeople together and explained that the Tartars could arrive at any minute. I ordered for all the carts and wagons to be pulled into the town square and for these to be filled with the people who were without any other means of travel. The old, sick, and the children were loaded first. These wagons were instructed to leave straight away, as they would need three or four hours head start on the Tartars, in order to reach Jain Kang before them. Each wagon had one of my soldiers, as a guard.

People were trying to leave carrying their valuables, including heavy furniture! You'd think people would have more common sense than that. They were warned to leave their heavy positions behind; I knew that those who ignored my commands, would be the first to die.

Scouts were sent out to look for any signs of the Tartars. Time was running out, I was about to give orders to burn the remaining homes, but I felt the touch of Mae's hand.

"Beat, can I leave some surprises for the Tartars when they arrive?"

I thought that sounded good. A kind of welcoming present.

"Any thoughts as to where your surprise should be?"

"We can dig holes and fill with some of my black bombs. Also on the road leading south."

"That's good. Plus, some of the main buildings." I added.

It had been a long day, and it was getting dark. I was still sitting in my saddle when I dozed off. I drifted into a dream; some people may say it was a daydream.

My thoughts had drifted to the Capital. We would not be able to prevent 500,000 Tartars reaching the capital. Including the Jin Soldiers, we would only have 300,000 against 500,000 Tartars. I was confident that my army's superior fighting skills would provide a victory for our combined armies. But the reason I could not order such an action was because of the cost in lives. Such an encounter would lead to a slaughter. The Eastern army would lose maybe half its soldiers.

In my dream I was reminded that the Capital of the Eastern Jin was beside the sea. In fact, on one side of the city there were cliffs. I dreamt of a moat from the Sea, surrounding the city. If the timing was right, a lot of Tartars could be killed when the sea was released, and the moat could protect the City from them.

I ordered Mae and Marcus to take fifty men and ride to the Capital and build a moat. I showed them a drawing of my plan.

As they rode west, I sent Anthony with ten soldiers to find the Western Jin and the Northern Jin. They were to Inform them that I would have

200 Roman soldiers ready to drive out the Tartar warriors. We would be at Jain Kang and if they joined us, maybe we could drive the Tartars out of China forever.

Then the bad news arrived. My scouts returned, and they brought news that the Tartars were approximately six hours away.

There were still people running around collecting their possessions. I had warned them that they had to escape. Now. With or without their valuables. Otherwise, they would all be killed when the Tartars raped and pillaged their town. I ordered all the remaining soldiers to each pick up one of the townspeople and take them back to the Capital. There was little more I could do to help them.

Two hours later, all my soldiers had left and were riding as fast as they could to the safety of my main army. I sat on my horse watching the remaining people running to and fro. There would be no escape for them. Some were the rich people who I met at their council offices; they were still trying to save as many of their possessions as they could.

The saddest part was that there were still so many of the peasants in the town. These people had very little to begin with, but many were carrying their last remaining things of any value. To us it would seem worthless, but to those who had next to nothing, it was all they had. The problem was, anytime now they would all be dead.

From the hill where I sat on my horse overlooking the town, I began to see clouds of dust. Half a million horses make masses of dust. Soon after, the first of the Tartars rode into town. I expected them to start the slaughter as soon as they arrived, but this was different. The Tartar warriors started to round all the people up. They were gathered outside the council offices.

Eventually the man who appeared to be their king, rode into the square. He dismounted and sat on the seat provided. First the town leaders were dragged before him. The valuables they had collected were torn from their grasp. They were lined up, and all of them were beheaded. What fools they were. If they had simply left their valuables behind, they could have been alive somewhere in the Capital at this moment.

Then this so-called leader called the poor people forward, one at a time. I have seen some barbarism in my life, but this took the biscuit. The first victim was an old man, he had nothing apart from his own life. He was laid on the ground, then his limbs were tied to four horses… I won't talk about the rest, there was too much gore. I felt physically sick.

I could not leave these poor people to suffer at the hands of this maniac. I had to do something to help them. I rode to the peak of a nearby hill, where I was visible from the town. I then shouted at the top of my voice.

"I am Commander Zug of the Eastern Roman army. How would you like a chance to fight me in hand-to-hand mortal combat? If you win, you will achieve great honour among your people. If I win, I will take all these people and leave in safety." I waited for maybe ten minutes in total silence, before the Tartar responded. Eventually he started to speak through his interpreter.

"Roman, it is true that I will receive great Honour when I kill you in combat. I could of course just have you captured now, and killed at my pleasure. But I am not a coward. I will receive the honour of killing you in combat." He boasted proudly. "If you, by some miracle, manage to kill me, then you and these hapless people will receive your freedom."

I dismounted and told my horse to hide somewhere, I did not want him ending up as the property of some Tartar. Then I was picked up by a Tartar warrior and given a ride into town. There I was unceremoniously shoved off the horse. I momentarily laid in the dust at the feet of the man who I presumed was their leader. I stood up and brushed myself down.

"So, what will the rules of combat be?" I asked.

His reply was instantaneous.

"Roman, the fight will be with knives, and there are no rules."

I sat on the ground, where I removed most of my armour. I started to wish that Sky, Leon and the special team were with me, but I was glad that they were not. Sky and twelve dogs, even if they were special ones, would have no chance against so many Tartars.

A giant of a man stood beside the man I had been speaking with. It turned out that I had been negotiating with a man named Timur, who had been speaking for their leader. The real leader was this giant now standing next to him.

"Let me introduce myself. I am Khasan, leader of this army. And I will be the one who will kill you today."

Now, I am five foot ten inches; this man must have been about six foot six inches. He was tall and very well built. I was now starting to feel sorry for myself. Would I never see Sky or Leon again? Then I glanced across at the group of women, men and children, all relying on me to save them. I held my head in my hands, I realised that I required a miracle to save myself and these people.

I have been in similar positions in the past. What action did I take? I prayed to the one who could deliver miracles. I was already sitting in the dust, so I just turned to a kneeling position, and asked Jesus for a miracle.

I was standing, knife in hand, at one side of the area designated for our fight. The other side stood a very confident Khasan. He charged across the space which divided us and was in front of me in seconds. I side stepped his first lunge.

"Stand still Roman, let me end this soon. My dinner is waiting!"

His next slash caught my shoulder, leaving a nasty cut. Next, he came in close and grabbed my hand which held my knife. I responded the same, and this resulted in him pushing me towards the wall, he was in fact trying to crush me.

I had to resort to the action which most ladies would use in this situation. I kneed him in the groin. Khasan bent forwards, I hit him on the back of his head with the back of my knife. He tumbled forward into the dust. At that point I should have plunged my knife into his back. But unfortunately, I was, and never will be, a wanton killer. Instead, I just stood and waited for Khasan to get back to his feet. A foolish move, I know.

He recovered quickly, and was soon back to slashing at me with that knife of his. This time he caught my chest as his blade passed by. I was now bleeding from my arm, and from a wound across my chest. I needed to end this quickly before I bled out. The next time he rushed at me, I ducked low and he ran into my shoulder. This was my chance, I pushed forward and lifted him over my back. Boy was he heavy! Khasan crashed on the ground behind me - that weight working in my favour. I turned and kicked his knife out of his hand, then jumped on top of him. He may have been muscular, but my muscles were more toned. It was a hard life alone on a mountain in winter. I was lucky, he was laying on his front when I landed on him. Pulling his head backwards, I was able to plant my knee onto the back of his neck. I pulled his head back hard, slowly moving my knife hand towards his neck. He shouted out in pain, then slapped the ground, crying that he surrendered.

I released him and got to my feet. For a few minutes I looked down at him, before I spoke. The once mighty leader of this army, was now crying in the dust. I turned to Timur.

"I have defeated your leader. The townsfolk and I are free to leave." As I finished my sentence, I heard a sound behind me. My body was still in a heightened state of awareness and my reflexes kicked in. I spun around and with the Khasan right in front of me, I plunged my knife into his chest. He fell to the ground dying.

There was a mighty shout from the watching Tartars. Many began rushing towards me. Not to praise me, but to kill me.

"Stop!" A loud shout came from Timur. He now seemed to be the leader of this army. Timur came to where I was still standing.

"Roman, you have killed our leader. You have won your freedom, and that of these people. Take them now and depart. You have a three-hour head start, then my warriors will chase you. They wish to avenge their leader and I shall grant them that chance."

I thanked him and asked if we could at least have some transport for the people, as they would not be able to walk far. Timur waved his hand and wagons were brought forward. The Tartar warriors drove the people towards the wagons.

"Roman, I have become a leader today because you were able to kill Khasan." Timmur said quietly, away from his men. "For this, I thank you."

I called my horse who had kept himself as near to me as was safe. Then I rode off with the wagons full of people.

"Remember Roman, three hours then my warriors will be in pursuit." I turned and waved, with a smile on my face. In another time and place, perhaps we could have been friends.

CHAPTER TWELVE

THE SIEGE OF JIAN KANG

All the townsfolk had managed to squeeze into the four wagons. I led the way, and we all set off at a canter. We only had three hours head start on the Tartars and the wagons full of people would be slow moving.

I turned the situation over and over in my mind. I could ride off at speed and hope to be able to bring some kind of help back. But the problem was that I had no idea what sort of help I could bring. At first, I was riding at the front of the column. Then I realised that I should be at the back a mile or so behind, in order to give an early warning, if the Tartars were approaching. We had travelled for about six hours; the horses were starting to tire. There was no way we would make it back to the capital before the Tartars caught up. About half the passengers were men. I stopped the wagons. I ordered the men to get out and explained that I wanted them to hide in the forest that we were passing. To hide there, then I would return for them after defeating the Tartars. This would lighten the wagons, and give the women and children more chance of arriving at the capital before the Tartars. They agreed, saying quick goodbyes to their loved ones, and quickly disappeared into the woods.

The wagons now picked up speed, but the odds were still on the Tartars catching us. I started to query my vision. There appeared to be clouds of dust in front of us. I rubbed my eyes, and looked again. It was what I thought I had seen. The Tartars were behind. Unless some had circled us and were now in front as well. Then my heart skipped a beat. It was Sky, with her warriors. She dismounted and ran into my army.

"Beat, you're still alive! How did you escape?"

I told her that I would explain things later, but we had thousands of Tartar warriors not far behind. She shouted orders to her warriors, to give all the women and children a lift on their horses. After setting fire to the wagons, we all galloped off to the capital, to safety. I say safety, but with half a million Tartars rushing towards the city, it may not be that safe.

As we came into sight of the city, I looked for a moat. From where I was seated, I could not see one. As soon as I was near the walls of the city, I dismounted and ran up to Mae.

"Mae, why isn't the moat ready? The Tartars are not far behind us." Mae then explained that she was acting according to my orders.

"You ordered me to build a moat using the strength and skills of the peasants, rather than sacrificing them in battle".

"That's correct."

"Therefore, I have carried out this order, come with me," I was practically dragged to the edge of the moat. "There is your moat!" The peasants worked day and night digging this, it's built to the measurements you ordered."

"But what about the water?" I asked.

"Were you hit in the head? Has your memory been affected? You ordered me not to flood the moat until the Tartars are in the process of crossing, so the water will drown many of them when the moat is filled."

I gave Mae a big hug.

"Mae, I am sorry. I have been under some pressure of late. Please forgive me. You have done an amazing job." Mae accepted my apologies. Then up popped Sky.

"I am still waiting for *my* hug, and the explanation as to what happened at the town?"

The hug and a kiss I gave her immediately, then we sat for a while as I explained what happened in the town. Mae had truly done a magnificent job. The moat was organised and she had three drawbridges built. Also, many of her black bombs had been buried in the fields surrounding the moat.

Then I saw him, my best friend. How I had missed Leon! He was rushing to me at full speed, followed by ten, now full-grown, pups. I had forgotten to move when Leon rushed forward and crashed into me - I was flattened, and he was laying on top of me licking my face.

I was just getting my breath back, when the second tidal wave hit. Ten pups, almost the size of their dad. Lucky for me, their mum Beaue came to my rescue. After she had driven her pups off me, I felt that I had just fought the whole Tartar army. But I wouldn't change anything.

"Beat, the pups are full grown now, shouldn't we name them?"

"Yes, I think we should, although I am a bit busy at present, preparing for a visit from half a million Tartars. How about you think of girls' names, and I will come up with boys' names. Don't forget to discuss them with Beaue." She gave a big smile then ran off.

Now, back to the siege. The draw bridges were all still down, with a lot of activity going back and forth. Tons of food had been stored in the city, along with gallons of fresh water. I had thousands of arrows made. I would keep my army safe behind these walls.

I wanted to leave scouts outside to give me some idea as to what the Tartars were planning. The problem was, how can you hide scouts among 500 thousand savages? Then it came to me. I couldn't send human scouts, but I could send my special team.

I was jumping for joy as I walked across to Leon and the gang. They were half way across the drawbridge when we finally met up. I explained what I wanted the special team to do. Leon was very excited; this would be far better than lying about in the city. A bit of adventure!

Leon was big even for his breed, but one of his pups was slightly taller than even Leon. His name was Saxa. I guess I couldn't exactly call them pups any more, as they were all full grown. Saxa, the largest of Leon's litter, appeared every bit a leader himself. I believed that Leon would begin to rely on Saxa more and more.

All the dogs, on hearing my plan, rushed across the drawbridge, and disappeared for a few days.

Next, I set up a meeting with my war team. I also included Emperor Yuan in the meeting, not because he was an Emperor, but because he was putting 100,000 of his soldiers under my command.

The plan was to line the walls with as many archers as possible. During the Tartar attack, the archers would fire thousands of arrows into the Tartar warriors. Before that, a team of my best fighters would have the task of blowing up the dam which was keeping the sea out of the moat. The dam would be blown when the moat was filled with as many Tartar warriors as it could hold.

Mae has worked with her own team, which had also buried lots of her black bombs in the fields surrounding the city. I would say we were as ready for the Tartar attack as possible.

Later, my scouts started to return.

"Bad news I am afraid sir," came the first report, "The Tartars are maybe an hour's ride away."

Other reports were similar, apart from one bit of good news. They had no form of siege engines. So, how were they intending to break into the city?

Then it finally happened. There was so much noise and smoke, it was total chaos. There was no attempt to raise their tents, or prepare a camp in any way. All the Tartars rushed towards the city. They, of course, were all riding their ponies, and rode straight towards the moat. When their stocky ponies were riding at full speed, there was little that could be done to stop them. Thousands were toppling into the moat.

My orders had been to dig a deep, wide moat, so that anyone who fell in would have difficulty climbing out. The Tartar warriors were falling on top of each other. Their generals finally saw what was happening and sent hundreds of officers to try and stop the disaster. They were like lemmings, charging to their deaths. It was time to signal the team to blow the dam. The team consisted of Anthony, Kuuli, and Deana (who had insisted on going. Then Acilla had also asked to be included. I agreed for all of them to go. Mae had packed lots of black powder under the rocks. There was a line of black, powder running from under the rocks, to the place where they were all hiding.

Unknown to me, Timus had sent scouts ahead of his main party. It wasn't much later when more clouds of dust appeared. The idea was that as soon as the moat was filled with the sea, my little band would then swim across the moat.

I gave orders for the Dam to be blown, by having a burning arrow fired into the sky. Deana was the first to notice - twenty of the Tartar scouts had seen them, and were running towards them. They are all brilliant fighters, but four against twenty wouldn't give them much of a chance. Also, if the dam wasn't blown, then the Tartars would eventually get to the gates to the city and break in.

My friends were fighting back-to-back, many of the Tartars were lying dead on the ground, but they were taking various cuts and stab wounds. Then six of the scouts drew their bows - they had decided to end fighting with swords - to fill my team with arrows. I was watching the event from the walls of the city. I felt so helpless. There was nothing I could do to save them. Anthony, my friend Kuuli, I was not sure what I would tell Deana's Father - I had promised to bring her home alive. And young Acilla, she was too young to die. I felt like a man with his hands tied behind his back.

Sky joined me, she could see what I was looking at and soon realised what was happening.

"What are you going to do, Beat?"

I had no answer to her question. All I could do was just watch four of my best friends die.

Then for a moment I thought I saw something move behind the archers. And no, my eyes weren't playing tricks, I did. I had forgotten about them!

The archers never got to fire their arrows. In fact, all the scouts were soon removed from the fight. Kuuli was holding Deana in his arms, doing his best to protect her from the arrows. Anthony was doing the same with Acilla. They had their eyes closed waiting for the finality of death. They stood for a while, just waiting. After a few minutes, they wondered why they were still alive. Then instead of arrows striking their bodies, lots of hot wet tongues started to lick them.

I was leaning against the wall. Tears filled my eyes once again. Leon and his special, amazing, wondrous team had come to the rescue. He was standing back from his team and looking at me, as if to say "it's ok, I am here for you". I could swear he was smiling.

After Leon decided that they had finished the rescue, he called his team (I can't say pups any more - they were all full grown now) and they all disappeared into the woods.

Kuuli rushed over and lit the line of black powder. About a minute later there was a huge explosion. Rocks were flying all over the place. Then the sea crashed into what was basically a deep ditch. The moat was filled in a very short time. Leaving thousands of bodies, both men and horses, floating in the moat. They may be my enemies but I hate death, wherever I encounter it. It would be difficult to count the number of casualties, but it was enough to make a big hole in the Tartar army.

Deana and Kuuli, were sitting with their arms around each other, it was hard for me to believe they may have died twenty minutes ago, I couldn't imagine what they were feeling. Something else was also going on though - Anthony and Acilla were sitting next to each other, in deep conversation. I wondered what they had found so interesting to talk about, and in the middle of an intense battle no less! The four of them waited for the flood to settle before swimming across to the spot I had arranged to meet them at.

I stood on the walls of the city, trying to anticipate what Timus would do next. His options were limited. He did not have any siege engines, so propelling any form of missile against the walls of the city would not happen. Build rafts to cross the moat? Well, that was an option but I would send burning arrows into the flotilla and that plan would not last long. Starvation was a possibility. The problem would be that we were prepared for a long siege and had large stocks of food and water, plus hay for our horses. We would be sitting comfortably inside our walls whilst he had a massive army to feed. He only had two options. He could send men across the moat and hope that they could set fire to the gates. Or hope I would be stupid enough to send my army out to fight him. Which wasn't going to happen.

While Sky and I waited for Timus to decide on his course of action. We decided to name the pups.

All groups, whether people or animals, have members with different characteristics. There will always be one who is clearly the leader. Females often produce a matriarch. One is often a bit of a character, sometimes called the 'clown'. A few will have leadership qualities; however, most will be followers.

Sky named the girls. The one who she felt was the Matriarch, was given the name Frida. She was more than capable of caring, or chastising, both sexes. Inga was the name given to the girl who was the most adventurous. The strongest was clearly Auda - none of the girls would challenge her.

That also includes a lot of the boys. Goda, gentle Goda, she was a kind and loving dog. One who was happy laying in your arms being stroked. Next, we come to the boys. First of course is Saxa, he was a copy of his father - Leon 2.0. Roza was a crafty boy, if you ever needed someone to remove something from… let's say a house, then he was the boy for the job. Now Judda, he was also leadership material. A backup for Saxa. His second in command. The strongest was Agi, dare I say it, even stronger than Leon at his best. Then we have Alard and Bada - both loved the water, when it comes to swimming, not many dogs could swim faster. Leon and Beaue had the perfect pack to follow them.

Timus had a big problem… How was he going to feed his army, if he got involved in a long siege? At present he had his warriors searching for miles to find food and fresh water. His problem was that I had got Sky to collect all the food and fresh water nearby and bring it inside the city walls. What we could not bring inside, we destroyed.

It was pitiful watching the horses being killed for food. After a month the men started to die.

Timus played his last card in order to try and regain some honour. He challenged me to a hand-to-hand combat. If I won, he would leave with his army. If he won, the Tartars could enter the city unopposed. He must have thought I was stupid. When I fought Khasan in Badong, even though I won, his men wanted to kill me. Even when he let the people and I free, he then only gave us a three-hour start. At that point I remembered the men from the village we had left, hiding in the woods. I made a mental note to go back and collect them as soon as possible.

I leant over the walls and shouted.

"Your word is like mud. It is too soft and treacherous to be trusted."

Then I ordered a thousand more arrows to be fired. The five hundred thousand Tartar warriors were now reduced to about three hundred thousand sick and starving men.

I was suddenly attracted to what looked like animals up on a hill. I looked for a while, then realised that it was Leon and his team. He was trying to tell me something. We had communicated for many years.

Although we spoke different languages, we understood each other. Finally, I understood what he was trying to say. He was telling me that our reinforcements were coming. The Northern and Western Jin armies were nearby. This was it, what I had been waiting for. I gave the orders to get the soldiers ready.

My light cavalry would charge out first, firing arrows before they drew their swords. Then the heavy cavalry would follow. Finally, the foot soldiers would do what they do best.

About two hours later, they came into view. Our allies charged downhill and smashed into the back of their army. All three drawbridges were lowered. Then I heard the order for my army to do their bit. The Tartars were driven out of China.

There were big celebrations and plenty of food left from the stores, so we shared it all among us all.

Emperor Yuan promised me whatever I wanted. I told him that I was planning to take Mae back to her county. The emperor promised to make as many ships as I needed.

"Let's see... 1000 soldiers per ship. That's about 2000 ships."

Emperor Yuan looked at me and smiled.

"Ok. You used your soldiers to defend my Empire, I will use my peasants to build your ships."

CHAPTER THIRTEEN

HOME AT LAST

S hips do take some time to build, but this gave my army time to rest and recuperate. I met up with Lia and Marcus one sunny afternoon. I asked Lia if she had any plans for the future.

"When my sister and parents were killed, I felt that I had no reason to live. Then I heard that you were taking the army to Jerusalem. I found a reason to carry on. You gave me the role to check if all your soldiers were Christians. It was then that I met Marcus. As you know, Quintin was insisting on marrying me, and Marcus gave me a shoulder to cry on. He became my rock. Gradually, I fell in love with him."

Then Marcus began to speak.

"When I first met Lia, I saw a woman who was hurting. Despite her pain, she was always caring for others." He grabbed hold of her hand. "I have fallen deeply in love with Lia. I want to marry her." I told them that I was pleased to hear it.

They stood there with their arms around each other.

"Well then," I began. "I guess you may both be interested that we will be passing through Jerusalem on our way home…"

Lia grabbed hold of me, obviously excited by the fact.

"Beat, can we get married there?" I told her that, as I was the commander of the Eastern Army, her wish was more than possible.

Next, I wanted to speak with Deana and Kuuli. I left Lia and Marcus and went to where I expected to catch both of them. Who did I bump into? No other than my darling Sky.

"Where are you going honey?"

I told her that I was on my way to see Deana and Kuuli.

"I have just been chatting to them, my love. Why? Do you want to meet up with them?" I thought this would be a good time to tell her about Lia and Marcus. "Lia and Marcus are going to be married when we arrive back in Jerusalem."

She looked at me and started to laugh. "I know that, I was talking with them earlier. I have also spoken with Deana and Kuuli." I asked her what they had to say.

"Well, they have a problem. They are both in love, which I expect even you are aware of. They want to marry, but as Deana is a Ghassanid Princess, she will have to marry whoever her father tells her to. Also, as a princess, she will be expected to rule the tribe when her father passes on. When we arrive back in her city, she may have to stay there and be forbidden from seeing Kuuli ever again."

"Tell them that I will try to mediate for them, and not to worry. Love conquers all."

I also thought about how Anthony and Acilla were getting close... but that would have to wait. I needed a chat with Mae, it wouldn't be long before we set sail for her homelands.

I found Mae making more black powder. She had told me that she had been told how to make it in China, and there were plenty of the chemicals required to make more where they lived. Also, she felt that they may need some when we arrived in her village.

"Hi Mae, how are things going?" I asked. "Are you getting excited about seeing your family after all these years?"

Mae looked at me. I could see tears running down her face.

"I was kidnapped over five years ago. My little Adam will now be twelve. Axil will be thirteen, and my oldest, Aris, is now seventeen. He has grown into a man. Without me." She sobbed for a moment. "I can't wait to hold my husband in my arms again. It's been such a long time!"

"Well, I will leave you to your black powder making, and we shall have a longer chat on the ship".

I now had to check on how the ship production was progressing. It was late spring and I hoped to cross the South China Sea during the summer. I had heard that the beaches in Mae's homeland were beautiful in the summer. I was looking forward to spending a week or so there.

I met up with the captain of the Fleet.

"Captain, how are your men doing, can you give me a date for my ships to be ready to sail?"

The captain informed me that 25 ships could take a year to build. Then a smile came to his face.

"Commander, they will be ready to sail in two weeks' time."

I was so happy, I even jumped up and down a few times.

"I can't thank you enough captain." I then rushed back to give the information to my officers.

The two weeks went fast. I just had to make a final visit to Emperor Yuan. I had fallen in love with the people of Ctesiphon. I had also fallen in love with the people of Jian Kang. It would be hard to leave them, but I was sure Mae would provide a good case for leaving.

Before I finalised the boarding, I had to pay a visit to Leon. His team were lying about in the grass, enjoying the early sunshine. I went over to Leon and laid down beside him.

"So, my hairy brother, thanks again for getting us out of trouble at the dam." Leon knew what I was saying, he responded with several licks. "Leon, we used to spend all our time together, since you have had your family, we don't seem to meet that often". I then told him that in future I wanted his family to live next to my family, wherever we were in the world. That did it, Leon leapt onto me. Before he had the pups, it was just Leon on top of me. Now all his pups always followed him. Once again, Beaue came to my rescue.

Eventually everything was loaded, it was just the soldiers to board now. I had joined up with Sky, Deana, Kuuli, Lea, and Mae. The rest of my officers were busy with the loading.

We all boarded the same ship. While we waited for the ship to sail, we asked Mae questions about the South China Sea. I had only sailed on a sea once before. This was of course the Mediterranean. That, compared to the

South China Sea, was a pond. Mae explained that the sea was calm most of the time, but if there was a storm, then it would be a bad one. Then she pointed out some large fish with fins. She explained that these fish were called sharks. They were big, fast, and ate people. What a nightmare, I thought. I remembered diving in the sea to rescue Sky in the past. If I had to do it again, I would have one of these shark fish chasing me for its lunch.

I went to find the captain and asked him a few questions. There were two things of interest. Firstly, the emperor had ordered him to take us wherever we wanted to go, then wait for us to leave. Then take the army as far home as a ship could carry us. The second point was that we should arrive in a couple of days. I sent messages to the other ships, then spread the news around our ship. Mae was now getting very excited. She had waited five years to see her loved ones.

Gradually, our ship sailed closer and closer to the islands. They were surrounded by beautiful sandy beaches. If you went past the beaches, you'd get into what could only be described as massive tropical jungles.

The ships had to wait offshore. Landing was going to be a massively difficult project to undertake.

Men swam across to the beaches. They then cut trees, and the trunks were bound and pushed out across the sea to act as rafts.

We were one of the first rafts to disembark. Each ship unloaded its stores and horses, then the main body of my army started to disembark. We all started to walk up the beach in the direction of those giant trees which seemed to line the top of the beach. Suddenly a tall man came running onto the beach, shouting something to us, which I for one could not hear. Just behind him came three other runners carrying spears. The pursuers were closing on the lone runner.

"That's my husband!" Mae shouted, obviously very worried for him.

Three arrows whistled past my ears. The pursuers were now lying dead on the sand. The archers were Sky, Deana and Kuuli. Mae thanked them, then ran towards her husband, who was still running towards us.

It brought tears to my eyes. Two people in love, who have been apart for so long, finally embracing each other. Sky told me to leave them for a while, which I did, as unloading the ships was a priority. If a storm suddenly blew up, I could lose the whole fleet.

It took all day to complete the unloading of all the ships. We made a temporary camp at the top of the beach. This was the best plan; we would make future plans after I had spoken to Mae and her husband. When all the ships were unloaded, they sailed along the coast and anchored in a sheltered bay.

I woke early, as usual, with the sun barely a hint of light beyond the horizon. Sky was still asleep, we were all sleeping in the open, under the blue skies. I decided to wake Leon and go for a walk. Leon had obviously had the same thought and was on his way to me. When he was a pup, he would jump up on me when we met. Well, he still does this, which is a problem at times as he often knocks me over. So, I now try to dodge him. This time he did not miss me and I crashed onto my back. As I was laying there slightly stunned, a tall man approached us. He held his hand out to lift me off the ground. The man was strong, he pulled me up with ease.

"Please let me introduce myself, my name is Datu. I am the chief of this tribe and husband of Mae. Can I join you for your walk?" He then stroked Leon. Noone strokes Leon unless he accepts them as a friend.

"You are welcome to join us on our walk. Maybe you can answer some questions. In particular, if you are the chief of this tribe, where are your people?"

"These islands are inhabited by many tribes. Some small, some medium, and a few large tribes. Most of the time, we all live in peace. However, at present three of the four big tribes have united. They are now attempting to overrun all the other tribes." He spoke with sorrow in his voice. "Two days ago, they arrived at my village just as the sun was rising. We had no chance to defend ourselves. Many were able to escape into the jungle, but many were captured, including two of my sons."

I asked him if he knew where his people were being held. He knew exactly the place. I put my arm around his shoulders.

"My friend," I said, "Your people will be back in your village by noon tomorrow. We will attack your enemy and rescue your people early tomorrow morning." I then asked Datu, to bring his people out of the trees, my soldiers would protect them.

The villagers camped on the beach. with my soldiers surrounding them. Datu stood with his arms folded.

"I see you are a man of your word." He smiled.

What had become my gang, gathered with Mae and Datu. He warned Mae that the children had grown up a lot. He gave the bad news first, that was that the youngest, Axil, and Adam had been captured. Datu, then put his arm around Mae,

"This is our oldest son. Do you remember Aris? He is seventeen now, and I have a surprise for you."

Mae started to become concerned about this secret. Had Datu found another woman? Then all her worries came to a head - he was leading a young woman towards her."

Let me introduce Diwa, she is our adopted daughter. She is the same age as Aris. She lost both her parents, so we took her in"

Mae was visibly relieved.

"So, I now have a daughter?"

Mae put her arms around young Diwa, she indeed now had a daughter. Sky and I watched the new relationship unfold; it was heart-warming.

We got together with Datu to discuss the rescue of the missing people. I asked how many warriors were with the villagers. He thought there may be fifteen thousand, all on foot, they did not have any horses. It seemed that three tribes had gathered together.

"Have no fear my friend, I will send in my infantry soldiers, our only problem will be getting to the villagers, especially your sons, before they have a chance to kill them." I thought for a moment. "I have a plan. We need to have two rescue teams in place before the attack."

Team One: Myself; Sky; Lia; Marcus; Acilla (she insisted on coming); Beaue; Saxa (who would lead four of the other pups); ten-foot soldiers.

Team Two: Datu; Mae; Deana; Kuuli; Leon; five pups; ten-foot soldiers.

As soon as Datu saw my list, he complained.

"I am not taking *either* woman… Maybe Deana if you insist, but my Mae is too weak for this. My Mae is good at looking after the family. This is men's work."

Maybe the Mae who was kidnapped five years ago would have accepted this from her husband, but the Mae who I have brought back to him would certainly not!

She pushed past me and stood in front of her husband. He was in trouble now, Datu may be a good foot taller than Mae, but she was now a seasoned warrior. I had seen her fight against Tartars, Huns, and Sassanid soldiers, without ever being defeated. All these opponents were better fighters than anyone on these islands, even her husband.

"Husband, if you want me to stay here and do your washing, prove you are a better fighter than me."

Datu laughed.

"Ok, I chose swords, then hand to hand combat."

Mae smiled.

"Get your sword then. I carry mine all the time" Datu looked surprised, why would his wife carry a sword with her? And why would she be serious about fighting him?

My soldiers formed a square. Datu and Mae moved around the ring, sizing each other up before making the first move. Then Datu rushed across the ring and pretended to try and hit Mae.

He still had not realised who he was fighting against. Mae sidestepped the sword thrust, and slapped Datu across his buttocks. Datu was furious, he turned and again rushed at his wife. This time Mae was past playing, their swords tangled and, in a flash, Datu had lost his sword.

"My dear husband, are you ready for the hand-to-hand combat?" Datu was now very angry and fairly humiliated. His face was quite red.

"Of course, I am ready, dear wife. As I am at least a foot taller than you, shall I fight with just one hand?" Mae thought a bit before answering.

"You are good at talking, but when are you going to fight?"

Datu had still not learned his lesson, he again rushed towards her. Mae grabbed his arm, turned her hip and Datu was lying on the ground. He sprung up, embarrassed. Again, he charged Mae. Again, he finished on the ground. I shouted that one more fall would decide the winner. This time Datu took his time. They seemed to be stalking each other. Datu was planning to get in close, grab hold of her and then pick her up and hug her until she submitted. beginner's lesson. He did get close; he did manage to grab one of her arms. In a flash she grabbed his arm, and after a couple of movements, Datu was lying on his stomach with one of his arms being pushed up the middle of his back - which looked very painful. He had no choice but to give in. She helped her husband up.

"You were lucky my love, both Deana and Sky are better fighters than me. Let me take you home and give you some of the TLC we haven't shared for the last five years."

Datu was both annoyed and embarrassed, but this offer, he approved of and the two of them went off in each other's arms.

I was about to grab hold of Sky and find somewhere to have a rest before our late-night venture, when an old lady approached me.

"Sir, are you Beat?" She asked.

"Yes, ma'am." I replied.

"I am Mae's grandmother. My husband and I have not eaten for maybe five days, most people here are starving." I turned to a nearby soldier, and I ordered him to provide some rations for this lady immediately. I told her that I would speak with Datu later, regarding the other villagers.

"Young man, has Mae told you about the hidden enemy? They are more of a danger to your army than the other tribes."

I told her that I had not had time to speak with Mae since coming ashore.

"The biggest killer in these Islands are the Mosquitoes. You must provide nets to cover your men at night." She warned, carrying on. "There are also venomous spiders. And watch out for the scorpions. Not to mention there are fourteen poisonous snakes on the islands. The spitting cobra is the most dangerous. If your men want to swim in the sea, watch out for jellyfish and bull sharks - they swim in saltwater and freshwater, so can also be found in the rivers. Also, there are crocodiles that can grow to twenty feet." She paused for a moment, just as I was about to reply she continued. "I see that you have some beautiful dogs. You must keep them close and protect them. There are so many rabid dogs on these islands that often dogs are killed, mostly just in case they have rabies."

I waited a little longer to respond this time, but this time she seemed to have finally finished.

"I give you my thanks for the warnings. We will get our job done then leave the Island as soon as possible.

Sky was with me and even she was worried.

"Where are we going to get nets for over 200,000 soldiers, plus the horses?"

"That's a good question, I am afraid the answer is we can't, let's finish our work here as quickly as possible and leave."

I had been told that it was a two hour walk to the enemy camp. So, we gathered at 4pm. The plan was that I would take all the foot soldiers with us. When we were maybe a twenty-minute walk from the camp, the rescuers would move towards the enemy. As soon as the sun rose, the rest of the infantry would charge. Therefore, we had to free the captives, then stand and protect them until the infantry arrived.

Both teams gathered for instructions. Leon and Saxa were rubbing themselves against my legs. Mae and Daku were near the front, I could see that they had spent a few happy hours together. They were holding hands and they both had massive smiles on their faces. Daku seemed to have forgotten his embarrassment.

"You two!" I shouted, "Enough of those holding hands stuff." They both let go of each other's hands, and saluted. I burst out in laughter and they soon followed suit.

Both groups were off, with Leon leading his group and Saxa leading my group. The reason I took Saxa instead of Leon, was that I wanted to see just how good Leon's son was. One thing was for sure, Saxa had a lot of belief in himself.

Saxa took his siblings to the left, they would remove any sentry's. He knew that his dad, Leon, would take the rest of his family to the right.

As soon as the sentries were removed, both groups moved towards the area where the captives were being held. They had been split into two groups. One group were the under twenties, the second group were the over twenties.

"That's helpful, one group for each of us".

Then I saw that each group of captives were guarded by twenty warriors. We could not just charge the guards, as the villages would be dead long before we arrived. I sent Judda to his father, to tell him that I wanted the villagers rescued. Only Leon would understand my command. Then Saxa set off with his team to perform a rescue with the other group, the under twenties. Leon's pups had no problem crawling close enough to the captives to make a quick sprint to get to them when the guards weren't looking. As soon as the captives were freed, we rose up from the ground where we had all been waiting for our chance to move in. Twenty warriors were no problem to my soldiers.

Next, we just had to defend them until our main army arrived. Each group of fifty captives had to be protected. Soon I was among the rival villagers. Each team had nineteen defenders, including Leon and his family. Both teams were facing overwhelming odds. This is what they train for. We held for ten minutes, until we finally heard my army arriving. The good news was that none of my soldiers were killed. The captives were surrounded by my men. My teams fought with their backs against the villagers. It took maybe five more minutes before the infantry arrived. When highly trained roman soldiers attack, others run.

We were soon back in camp with the rescued villagers. I found young Adam and Axil; they were unharmed. I took both of them to Mae and Datu. It was a magic moment when all the family were hugging together again. The happiest mother in the world at that moment, had to be Mae.

CHAPTER FOURTEEN

AN EXCITING REVELATION

I asked Datu if he had any ideas about how to create permanent peace on the islands. He could not help. So, I had a meeting with my main two advisors, Sky and Leon. I know Leon doesn't speak any known language, but he is very good with his body language. All three of us sat on the grass, eating some biscuits. Sky thought that it would be a great idea to hold a meeting with all the tribal leaders.

It made sense to me, so I set a date for the meeting. Envoys were sent to every tribe; I backed the envoys up with a hundred riders from my heavy cavalry to stop any potential funny business.

I was speaking to Lia about how Mae had seen many things on her return to these islands.

"When Mae was kidnapped, this was the only world she knew. But since then, she has experienced life in many more forward-thinking countries. I owe a lot to Mae; I don't suppose you could have a woman-to-woman chat with her please?"

Lia, held my hand.

"Beat, I have been thinking the same as you, she has been through a lot. When my parents were killed, I inherited a lot of money and land. I would love to give Mae and her family a piece of my land that they could farm. Of course, I would provide the animals and equipment as well, and education for her children. From my point of view, we could be close friends."

I thanked her, and asked her to let me know Mae's response. As I was walking back to Sky, I was approached by a talkative young man. I thought that I recognised him, but it would not come to me.

"My name is Aris; my mother is Mae. Could I have a word with you please?"

I placed my hands on his shoulders.

"Your mother has saved the lives of many of my soldiers. If I can help her son in any way, please just ask".

I now placed my arm around his back and led him to a secluded part of the beach, where we sat on the sand. Leon ran up and laid down beside me, followed by Saxa. I looked at Saxa and asked him what he was doing here. He just rolled on his back. What kind of answer was that?

Aris told me that he wanted some support from me.

"Will you teach me how to use the Bow, and the sword? I also need to learn about martial arts". I nodded and he looked down for a moment, as if feeling a little guilty for his next question. "I also want to join the Roman army."

I stood in silence for a while.

"Aris, I can grant all your requests, but only if your parents agree with them."

Young Aris shook his head.

"They won't agree, I am needed here to work. Like my brothers will be when they are a bit older." He then looked into my eyes.

"Let me tell you what life here will offer me and my brothers, and similar for Diwa. We all wake when the sun rises. Adam and Axil start their day by feeding the animals and I go with Diwa to the river to collect water. The river has crocodiles lurking under the water or in the bushes. Venomous snakes are often found near the river. Simply collecting a jar of water could cost us our lives. We then eat some maise, boiled in water, before we start the real working day.

I go hunting with dad and we try to catch anything that moves. The prize kill would be a carabaos, but these are powerful, and fast. Many hunters are killed by them. Our spears often just bounce off their skin.

The family will work from sunrise to sunset, then we sleep. But our sleep is fear ridden - mosquitoes are always a threat. No one in the village has any protection from them. Mum may say that I could get killed in the army, but at least I would have a chance to defend myself. Here I have no chance. It's all just luck."

Once again, I sat in silence, running my hand through Leon's coat.

"Aris, I promise to do what I can. But in the end, it's up to your parents. Ok?" He understood and wandered off with a wave towards me.

Sky had been watching, and of course listening.

"That's a sad story my love. What are you going to do?"

For a moment, that question stuck in my mind. Every query or problem was laid at my door. If I didn't come up with an answer, people would suffer. Sometimes this can be a heavy load. I leant forward and held my face with both my hands.

"Do you think all problems are for you to solve? Or is there someone who can take your problems, and give you peace."

I looked at her. She was so wise

"Yes. Of course. Jesus said, give your problems to him. Let's ask him for help."

I began to pray. Afterwards I felt so much better.

"Ok Sky, let's go and collect Lia, we have a job to do."

About an hour later, Sky, Lia and I were sitting beside Mae and Datu.

"Mae, we have become good friends during your time with us. Will you let me share some things with you both?" Mae looked at her husband, then gave me a nod.

"We know that Mae has experienced a different kind of living while with us. I won't explain what I am trying to say, but I am sure she understands. Today Aris asked if he could have a chat with me. He told me about family life here on the islands. About all the wild animals and dangers everyone here faces daily. He said he faces the possibility of death each day, just to get a drink of water. Education and self-improvement are not an option for him and his siblings. He asked me to teach him to fight. I can teach him to use a bow, Sky is the best with the sword, and his mum is best at martial arts. However, his main request was for me to let him join the army."

I handed the discussion over to Lia.

"Mae, when my family were murdered, I inherited all their wealth. I have lots of land in Italy. If your family wants to return to Rome with us, I will give you a large amount of land, for you to start a farm. I will provide animals, and tools. Also, I can send your children to school, and get them a good education."

I ended the conversation.

"It's up to you all. Think about it and let me know. I plan to leave these islands in a months' time."

When all the leaders of the various tribes had gathered, except for the Semestral, who had chosen not to attend (which was a shame as they were the largest tribe, they were also rumoured to be cannibals). The meeting started. I spoke first.

"My honoured leaders, I bid you all welcome. At this moment in time, I could lead my army around the islands and crush every tribe. That would end all wars on these islands. But upon leaving, I'm sure the wars would simply break out again. Force is not the solution. I believe that these silly wars of yours can be ended 'til the end of days. I am offering to support all of the tribes. I will provide spears and bows and teach your men to kill their prey with arrows to minimise risk. I will teach them how to grow crops and farm fish. I will help them to make their own tools."

The meeting ended with the tribes promising to send one man and woman from each tribe. They would be taught how to make tools and weapons. Everyone was happy with the outcome of this meeting.

"What about the tribe that refused to attend this meeting?" Called someone from the crowd.

I responded by standing and making a promise that all the training would be completed before we left. I called Marcus over and ordered him to take half the army and explain why they have to change their ways. I also asked Marcus to take Aris with him, to take him under his wing.

Marcus was proud of being asked to take Mae's son under his wings. He had an hour or two free, so he sent a soldier to bring Aris to him.

"Please sit beside me young Aris." Before carrying the request Aris asked why.

"I am taking half of our soldiers south to where the Semental tribe live. They never came to the meeting with all the other tribal leaders. Now I have to pay them a visit and basically ask them why they have been bad boys." Marcus chuckled lightly. "If you were the general in charge of this mission, what action would you take?"

Aris thought for a while before replying to the question.

"I think that people only really respect power. Small tribes respect the power of the larger tribes on these islands. Therefore, if I was in charge, I would storm through their village, killing as we went. They would respect the power of Rome, and behave themselves."

Marcus held his head in his hands.

"Aris, you are confusing respect and power with ruling through fear. Respect is gained through love, not fear. Also, during this charge through the town, think about who would be killed. Would it just be soldiers? Or would children and babies also be killed? Let's look at it another way." Marcus held up his hands. "My right hand is love; my left hand is fear. Tomorrow when we arrive at the Semestral village. Would it be best to use my left hand or my right hand?"

"Your left hand of course! They will see the power of Rome, and be in fear of being destroyed."

Marcus thought again and changed track.

"A man has to mow a field. His master tells him that if it takes more than 2 hours, he will be whipped and branded. Another man is welcomed, his master praises him and simply tells him to do his best. Which man do you think will do better?" Aris thought for a while before replying. "The man without pressure will win."

"Close," replied Marcus, "the man under pressure may do better at first, but over time the man being praised will strive to work harder for his master continuously, whilst the man under pressure will likely grow hateful towards his master and will have no true wish to please his master. The Eastern Army would give their lives, not for Rome, but for Commander Zug. When our commander plans a conflict, his first thoughts are how to prevent his men being killed. There are thousands of generals who look for glory, and have no care for how many of their soldiers die. I can think of some generals, who if they had led our army on this action, at least half our soldiers would be lying dead."

Aris nodded at this, he seemed to be beginning to understand.

"If we approach the Semestral in love. There will be a higher chance of peace." Marcus finished. "Anyway, you are to stick to me like glue until our army leaves these Islands.

cܬ cܬ cܬ

Sky and I were living in one of the army tents, The Special Team were in the tent next to us. I called Leon and Beaue to our tent as I wanted a chat with them. I told them that they could both stay in our tent, or whatever lodging we stay at. They both seemed happy - they were rubbing against us. At that point Saxa entered our tent.

"What's up with him Sky?"

She laughed.

"He is jealous, he wants to be the leader. Just watch Leon."

I waited, then Leon was in his face. There appeared to be some kind of communication before Saxa slowly left the tent.

"I think Saxa will develop into a great leader. But not yet. Leon is still in charge at present." I said.

Early the following morning Marcus was ready to leave. Aris had been given a horse. It was the first time he had ridden a horse and he had to be given some basic training before they left off. He had been lent a Roman uniform. Mae and Datu stood watching their son. They had the look of proud parents.

On arriving at the Semestral village, Marcus ordered his men to surround it. Then he and Aris, with a thousand soldiers, entered the Village. Marcus had been with me a few years now. He understood how I thought. He and Aris sat with the leaders on the ground and were given refreshments. He carried out the whole left-hand, right-hand thing. They finally agreed to seal a deed.

They were pleased that Marcus had agreed to send our soldiers to help them make and learn to use bows, arrows to help them hunt their food as well as how to make tools to help them farm the land. With the manpower of my soldiers, they also erected a ten-foot fence around their village, which with the number of soldiers took barely any time at all. The purpose of the fence was to keep wild animals out of the village, including snakes. Marcus told them that Mae had agreed to train people in the use

130

of herbs (the skill she learnt from the old man in China), then send these skilled people to all the villages to provide medical support and pass on their new knowledge. When the work had been finished, Marcus brought the soldiers back to camp.

Sky had been visiting Mae a lot over the last few weeks. I was wondering what they were up to. Then after one of these visits, they returned to our tent together.

"Sky has something to tell you. As you have probably noticed, she has been visiting me a lot."

I told her that it had not gone unnoticed.

"Ok, I will leave you together now, Sky can break the news." Then Mae hurried out of the tent.

"Beat, my love, can we lay down together?"

We both laid on the ground and I put my arm around her. I was getting a bit worried, was my super fit wife ill in some way? She put her arm around me

"My love, I have some expectant news." Now I was totally confused. "The two of us are going to become three."

Now how can two become three, I thought. Then it hit me, albeit a little later than it should have. I looked at Sky, she smiled and nodded.

"You're pregnant?"

"I always thought you were a bit slow. But not this slow!"

All conversation finished at this point. We were in each other's arms, and sharing kisses.

"I am going to be a father!" A tear came to my eye as that fact sank in. "Wait a minute Sky, I have to tell Leon that we are both Dads now."

Sky and I visited Mae and Datu to give them the sad news that we would be leaving in one weeks' time. Mae stood up and started to speak.

"Beat, we as a family have discussed the kind offer that Lia made us. If the offer is still on the table, we would love to return with you, and make our home in Italy."

I looked at Mae, with a frown.

"Hmm… I may have to ask Lia again," I couldn't help the small smile crack through my face "Oh, what is this document?" I held out a land grant. "Lia said that she hopes you all enjoy a new life."

Mae snatched the contract and held it against her chest.

"I think you and your family had better start to pack." I winked at her. "By the way, tell Aris that I have enlisted him in the Roman army, in a new role. He is now an officer in training, working under the guidance of General Marcus. Part of his training will be to study in Rome, when he is not on duty.

CHAPTER FIFTEEN

RETURN TO CTESIPHON

Aris and his siblings decided to have one last walk around their village. It was the night before they were due to leave for a new life. Adam and Axil were lagging behind, Aris and Diwa were walking ahead. The only sound they could hear came from the animals of the night.

This was until three drunken soldiers came into view. They must have been drinking some local brew.

"Hey beautiful, do you want a cuddle?" shouted the soldier in front.

Aris stood in front of Diwa. Seeing this, all three soldiers drew their swords from their scabbards. Aris was unarmed, but he stood his ground. He would protect Diwa, whatever happened. Aris was staring at the soldiers, when he felt a warm arm brush against his arm. Both his brothers had joined him. At this point, Sky, Leon, Beaue and myself were also enjoying an evening stroll. We had just turned a corner past a bamboo house, when we were greeted with this scenario.

We stopped trying to assess the situation. Three boys putting their lives at stake in an attempt to prevent three drunken soldiers harming a young woman. I turned to Sky.

"These boys have plenty of guts."

Aris picked up a stick, while the smaller boys grabbed a handful of earth in each hand. Sky and I were about to send Leon and Beaue in, to even the odds. When who appeared? Yes! It was Mae. She had come to find her children.

"A full-grown woman, now that's more interesting" shouted one of the soldiers. She stood in front of her children facing the soldiers. Aris moved alongside his mother.

"I like that lad, he has guts." I said to Sky, stroking my chin.

The first Roman charged with a sword in his hand. He didn't get far before Mae put him on the floor. Followed quickly by the second soldier. Same ending, again Mae put him on the floor. The first one started to recover but Aris hit him with the stick he was carrying. It was then the opportunity for the third soldier to strike, he raised his sword, only to be met by Mae demonstrating her roundhouse kick.

It was the younger boys turn to join the encounter.

"Now we just need Datu to turn up," Sky joked, smiling.

"I presume you mean the shadowy figure over there?"

That was the last piece to complete the puzzle, Datu emerged from around the corner. All the family were there now. The funny thing that happened next, was all her children clambering around her. Begging her to teach them the round kick. Other soldiers arrived when they heard all the noise. I ordered the soldiers to be arrested.

"What do you intend to do with them, my love?" Mae had seen us and waved; I returned a thumbs up.

"These apologies for soldiers, will be executed. I have no place in my army, for drunkards who attack women and children".

Sky was a bit shocked at my reply.

"Are you sure? It seems a bit harsh." I was now looking at Sky, with a very stern face, "They were ready to molest and kill a woman and her children. If Mae had not arrived, they would have succeeded. What if we had to attack a village? Wine and mead may be available, would these self-same soldiers not attack the women and children in the village as they tried here? We do *not* attack women and children."

Sky nodded and lowered her gaze and apologised, ashamed that she had questioned my decision.

The next morning, all the ships were ready, and set sail at noon. I had agreed to sell the long route. The longer we were at sea, the less marching we had to contend with. The plan was to sail west, eventually arriving at the mouth of the Euphrates. From there we would march north to the city of Ctesiphon, and pay a visit to Quinton and Shirin. My only problems would be food and fresh water. This would mean landing in various countries. We would also need to pray for protection from storms. A bad storm could sink all our ships.

Marcus and Lia met up with Mae's children. Lia had arranged tutors for all the children, starting today. The younger boys, Adam and Axil, would be schooled in Rome on arrival in Italy and Aris will have the rank of trainee officer (so at present he couldn't issue orders). He would be taught on route, or in school while in Italy. On Mae's advice, Diwa was also given the rank of trainee officer. All the children would receive training, with the bow, sword, and in martial arts. Sky was the first trainer to appear.

"I will give each one of you a number after every session."

There was a stir among the watchers.

"What will the points be for?'" asked young Adam.

Sky smiled.

"The number represents how many seconds I would take to kill you, if I wanted to." All the children were now looking at each other.

I met up with the captain.

"Where do you think, we will need to land first? We will need to replenish our stores."

We had planned to sail South-West-West, across the South China Seas and land on the island of Suwarnadwipa (Sumatra in the modern world) and collect fresh water. Then sail northwest, up the Andaman Sea, to the island of Ceylon. After restocking, we would sail west across the Arabian Sea, and up the Persian Gulf. My army would disembark at the mouth of the river Euphrates. The captain agreed, but he had little knowledge about Suwarnadwipa.

I could see Leon and his family, they were laying on the deck, looking bored. I understood how they felt. We were only happy when our feet were on the ground. I went over and sat with them. I could see Sky teaching Aris; his two younger brothers were fighting each other with wooden swords. I decided to start teaching, I need some way to relieve my boredom. I made a bow for each of them.

"Hey, would anyone like to practise archery?" I never knew they could move as fast. I handed a bow and some arrows to each of the boys.

"First, I want you to know, even if you are small, light, unable to fight on equal terms with a sword, with a bow, you can be equal, or even better than, any of your enemies." I told them. "Ok, you hold the bow with your weakest hand and pull the string with your strongest hand."

I walked them through the basics of how to load an arrow, how to hold the bow and string, and how to aim. Then I made them practise for two hours. I finished with another hour, teaching them how to make a bow and arrows. I had to admit, they were quick learners.

"How are my fledglings doing?" I wondered where Mae had got to? "They may be your fledgelings, but to me, they are such quick learners. I think they will be playing a part in getting us safely back to Italy." I then asked her if she could talk with Datu. "He was a blacksmith, and I wondered if something could be made to either, project your black bombs, or maybe find a way for your black powder to project a missile." Mae replied by saying that it would at least be something to relieve the boredom.

After weeks at sea, someone finally shouted the word we had all been itching to hear.

"Land ahoy!"

There she was, the island of Suwarnadwipa. We found a bay to anchor, then I ordered the infantry to disembark and follow me. The cavalry was ordered to leave the ship and exercise their horses. Our mission was to find fresh water, and restock our food supply.

While my soldiers carried out my orders, Sky, Kuuli, Deana, plus Aris and Diwa, decided to explore this island paradise with me. The weather was humid, and in no time, we were all sweating profusely. Leon had also brought his team out; they needed some exercise as well.

We arrived at a large clearing. What an amazing sight beheld us. We were familiar with elephants, as we had ridden war elephants in India. But here we were watching elephants in the wild. They were free. Mums, dads, and lots of babies. Totally awesome. We wandered on through some giant trees when I suddenly made a signal for everyone to stop.

Hanging on the tree in front of us, apparently, was a hairy woman with two babies. They looked like primitive people. As we all watched, one of the babies lost its grip and fell from the branch. His mother was on the ground rushing to her baby as quickly as she could. All of us were watching in silence, willing her to get her baby back to the safety of the tree. This picture of mother and baby love, changed in a split second. A huge tiger had been concealed in nearby bushes. Just as the mother was able to grab the hand of her baby, the tiger was on top of her. Death soon followed. The tiger looked at the baby, still holding its mother's hand.

I was furious. I rushed towards the tiger with a sword in my hand. Leon saw the foolishness of my action, and ran after me. His thoughts were that if I was going to die, we would die together.

Lucky for both of us, Sky had kept her cool. She ordered everyone to fire arrows at the tiger. It must take a lot to kill a tiger, as it kept crawling towards me. He had gotten to within two feet from me when Diwa released her last arrow. She really was good. Her arrow smashed through its skull and into its brain.

I ordered my soldiers to carry the tiger back to camp. We headed back along the trail to camp. About a mile from camp, a large number of islanders appeared, as if from nowhere. First, they pointed to Leon and his family, and made gestures to their mouths. I looked at Leon.

"It looks like they want to eat your family."

Leon's response was a loud howl. To which the rest of his family joined in. The islanders then pointed to the dead tiger and made the same gestures. Deana asked if I was going to give them the tiger.

"Personally, I would not have a problem giving them the tiger, but in my experience as a soldier, to agree to this would be a sign of weakness. Which would then be followed by a full-scale attack. So no, I won't give them the tiger." I replied.

The islanders started to spread out, there were about forty of them. I ordered my patrol to do the same. The numbers were about forty to twenty-nine. First, I looked at Diwa, and pointed to a tree. She understood and rushed over and was soon sitting on one of the branches. I then reminded Aris to use the lessons I had taught him.

"Ok let's go. This is their first encounter with a Roman army, let's hope they learn from it."

The fight was short and sweet, once they saw that our skills and weapons were superior to theirs, they fled back into the jungle. We hurried back to the camp and set sail as soon as possible. My feeling was that we would soon see far more of these islanders.

As our fleet set sail from Suwarnadwipa, the beach that we had just vacated was covered with spear-waving natives.

The wind was blowing in our favour, the fleet was making good time as we continued our journey west. Perhaps a week later, we landed on a large island. I understood that we were not that far away from India and the Gupta Empire. This was confirmed sooner than I had expected, as my fleet sailed into what appeared to be a safe bay. At the dock, there were a large number of ships. The flag flying from their ships looked like the same flag that my friend Chandragupta used.

I ordered the captain to sail the ship as near to the beach as he could. Of course, he had to avoid the ships waiting to unload. When we were as close to the beach as possible, without sinking, I ordered those who wanted to visit the island to start swimming. Bada and Alard were on the beach first - those boys were great swimmers, I sometimes thought they should have been fish. Only my foot soldiers were left on board the ship, to prevent pirates.

The arrival of Romans raised a lot of interest. Soon we were greeted by soldiers. This could be interesting, I thought. Then a big bearded man pushed his way through the soldiers.

"I don't believe it!"

It was the emperor's captain of his guards. We hugged and exchanged greetings. It turned out that the Gupta trading ships were in port, loading trade goods. We spent the evening celebrating with the Gupta men. After a couple of days, we had replenished our supplies and were continuing our journey west, across the Arabian sea. Eventually my fleet was sailing northwest along the Persian Gulf.

Two days later we reached the mouth of the Euphrates. My army disembarked and set up camp. It was a sad time, as we waved farewell to the crew of the fleet. We had been together for some time, and I for one would miss them.

After a few days' break, we started our trek north along the Tigris, which flows adjacent to the Euphrates.

I was not sure if Emperor Quintin and Empress Shirin would welcome us. Two hundred thousand odd mouths to feed, plus the animals. One man must have been happy though - General Shahpur and his soldiers had ridden thousands of miles. They did our hunting and provided us with fresh water. They all deserved a long rest. Five miles outside the city, I paid my respects to the general and his men, and bid them farewell. Then I and a selected few, plus the special team, decided to become tourists and visit the city undercover. We split into two teams: Sky, Acilla, Aris, Mae, Datu and myself, then Marcus, Lia, Kuuli, Deana and Diwa. The Special team was split between them. The teams were told to mingle in markets, drinking places and similar recreation venues. We were looking for anyone who may be delivering negative thoughts about the Emperor and Empress.

We didn't hear anything negative, in fact many people were praising them. What we did see was schools, hospitals, homes for orphan children. Most impressive was the large building in the middle of the city. Its purpose was to provide work for those who could not find any. I believe that everyone should be entitled to three basic principles. One: food and water every day. Two: a roof over their heads, and a place to sleep. Finally: a job where they can earn an income.

We all arrived at the main gate of the palace together. Two guards approached us. When I informed them that we were all friends of the emperor, not only did they refuse us entry, but they had the guard turned out.

"This is a bit of a problem, my friends." Then the Special team came alongside me, as if to be asked if they should take the guards out. There were about a hundred soldiers in front of us, with their swords out of their scabbards.

"Captain, if I were you, I would withdraw my men, before they are all killed". I looked up to where the voice was coming from. It was Quintin. He was leaning over the palace walls; he had a big grin on his face.

"You finally returned Commander!"

"I see your eyesight is still working Quintin. Are you going to get these gates open? I haven't eaten for hours."

Emperor Quintin, learnt over the wall, and ordered the gates to be opened. As we trundled inside the palace, I heard a conversation between the emperor and the captain of the guards. Quintin had informed him that they only had a hundred men, and we would have killed them in a few minutes had it come to a fight.

Quintin had indeed learnt how to throw a lavish feast. We hadn't eaten such a good meal for months.

Marcus later caught up with Quintin.

"How is life treating you, my friend?"

Quintin thought before he replied.

"I just want to start by saying that I am pleased you and Lia are now a couple, you deserve each other." There was a short, slightly awkward pause before he continued. "When I accepted the offer to share the throne with Princess Shirin, I thought that she was a wonderful woman. Now we truly are in love with each other, we share the same thoughts and dreams."

Marcus then gave his thoughts.

"I am so pleased for both of you. The commander sent us to the markets and pubs before coming to the palace. Everyone we spoke with high regard and praised the good work you have both been doing here. I always believed you to be a good man." He then introduced Quintin and Empress Shirin to the rest of the team. "Quintin, you remember Leon, of course," Quintin nodded, "Well, he has a family now." Leon, Beauc and the ten, not so much puppy's, walked forward. Quintin knelt in front of Leon and rubbed his fur." So, Leon, you are a father now! Well, done mate, keep that Beat on his toes." to which he smiled (although not at Leon this time).

Mae, who had visited the palace in the past, took her family on a tour. Adam and Axil, managed to escape from the walk about. Their target was me. After searching most of the building, I was located.

They were almost begging me to continue their teaching. They explained that they were young, but wanted to fight. The best way, so they said, was by the use of the bow and arrow, as this would compensate for their youth. These boys could easily have sat in a wagon, and avoided any fighting, but here they were asking me to prepare them for battle, despite their lack of strength. I told them both to come with me.

"Lads, if you want to be experts with the bow, there is only one secret. The word is practice. We will continue your practice now, and on our journey to Deana's family, we will continue practising, every day.

Finally, we were ready to depart. I would now return my Ghassanad Princess, back to her father. Quintin told me to take my 50,000 soldiers stationed in Jerusalem, back to Rome. He would provide protection for the city.

As the sun rose, all my soldiers were ready to march. The next stop would be a challenge for my negotiation skills. I knew my friend King Frome, Deana's father, would want his daughter to marry royalty and be Queen after his death. But I also knew that she was in love with Kuuli. I had enough soldiers to decide the outcome, but that would not be right - this was between father and daughter.

CHAPTER SIXTEEN

THE RETURN OF THE PRINCESS

It had been a long, exhausting day. We made camp just as the sun was setting, I had wanted to travel as many miles as possible before making camp.

Sky and I stumbled into our tent, then falling onto the makeshift bed, we lay there for a while. If anything, we were overtired. Leon and Beaue had no problems, they were both asleep in the corner.

"Sky, you're a Princess. I wasn't royalty, and I expect your father wants you to rule your tribe when he passes on. So why did he not oppose our marriage?"

Sky smiled.

"Because, simply, he could see we were both in love. A love that nothing could break."

I thought for a while before giving my reply.

"So, if Deana and Kuuli could prove how strong their love was, her father may agree to their wedding?"

Sky held my face in her hands.

"People are all different, who knows how King Frome will react. Let's get some sleep. We have another long ride tomorrow."

The following morning, I ordered Anthony to take twenty soldiers and ride ahead to meet King Frome. I want to know how his mood was, and how things were in his town.

"When you have formed an opinion, send a soldier back with your report." I ordered.

We rode for most of the day, then I ordered an early halt. I wanted to set up camp early again, for two reasons. The first was because I was waiting for Anthony's report. Second, I wanted to chat with Deana and Kuuli. I arranged dinner for the four of us to be set up in my tent. Deana and Kuuli had been invited to join us. We all sat round the meal, which we ate in silence. We were all deep in thought.

"Deana, if your father forbids you from marrying Kuuli, what will you do?"

She took her time before replying.

"I am the daughter of a King, as his only child, I have no option but to obey his command." I looked at her face and posture. I could see that this action would break her heart. I then turned to Kuuli.

"What are your thoughts my friend?" Kuuli, is a man who would fight all the Huns on his own, if I asked him to. But at present, silent tears were running down his cheeks.

"I love Deana with all my heart, but I am a low born, I was not born to a royal family. I will have to stand back and watch the woman who makes my heart beat, marry some noble. I would have no choice but to wish her all the happiness in the world."

Now all four of us were crying. Sky then spoke

"I am a princess; Beat is not royalty. And my father will expect me to rule my tribe after he passes on. My father saw in Beat, the man who he wanted for a son-in-law, and he gave us his blessings. So, nothing is impossible".

"If your father had rejected Beat, would you have disobeyed your father?" Deanna asked.

Sky was silent for a while, then replied.

"You must always follow your heart. Yes, I would have disobeyed my father. I could not have lived a life without Beat, even if I was a queen. Beat is my life."

The tent fell into silence. Deana was the first to leave, followed by Kuuli. I turned to this wonderful woman who I was lucky enough to find, and held her in my arms. I was not sure if this chat would help me to resolve the situation, but it was a start.

I heard a horse gallop up outside my tent, then someone dismounted and entered. It was one of Anthony's riders. He saluted smartly. Sir, I have a message from General Anthony. I accepted the message and told the soldier to get some food and have a rest.

The message was very interesting. King Frome was a worried man. The nearby kingdom of the Lakhmids was causing problems. He would be exceptionally pleased to see the Eastern army arrive in his town. When Deana heard this, she implored me to let her take soldiers and ride ahead to her father. I refused her request. I told her that if she wanted to act on impulse, she could of course take her two thousand warriors with her and I would be in her town in a couple of days. Deana looked at me, she was not happy with my response.

"Beat, my father lent you two thousand warriors. Is this how you repay us?" I looked her in the face.

"Deana, when Sky's father accepted me into his family. It is true, I was not royalty. But I was a Roman general. Roman generals are more powerful than most royalty. As the commander of this army, it would be foolish of me to just charge towards your father's town. I will meet you there."

She turned and rode over to her warriors, then waved her arms in the air in a signal for them to follow her, and off they went.

Kuuli rushed into my tent demanding to know where Deana had gone? Sky entered the tent with Leon and Beaue.

"What is going on?" asked Sky.

I updated her on what was happening. Kuuli grabbed her arm.

"Sky, please get Beat to give me 50,000 soldiers so I can follow Deana."

Sky was not happy. She just knelt down and threw him over her shoulder. He was laying on his back dazed. For a minute, Kuuli had forgotten that Sky was his princess. Kuuli was now embarrassed, and apologised. If this had happened back at the tribe, he would have received a death sentence. Sky held out her hand.

"Grab my hand, let me help you up".

What Kuuli hadn't noticed was that both Leon and Beaue were now standing in the corner ready to spring. No one attacked Sky or myself, while they were around. I quickly stood between Sky and Beaue.

"It's ok, stand down."

Beaue was showing her teeth, but Leon calmed her down.

Kuuli was ordered out of the room, while Sky decided on his punishment. Sky and I poured each other a goblet of wine.

"Beat, Kuuli has saved my life many times, and I know he acted out of love for Deana. I can't order his execution."

I thought for a while before replying.

"I have an idea, my love. Kuul, as a member of your tribe, could be executed. Also, he is not royalty or anyone of importance." She could not disagree. "So how can I resolve the situation?" I had come up with a possible solution. "Sky, would you say that Kuuli is brave, intelligent, and a good leader?"

She smiled.

"I would agree with all of that, why what's your plan?"

I scratched my neck.

"Well, I have to replace General Quintin. As your personal bodyguard, would Kuuli have any rank in your tribe?"

Sky thought for a while.

"He would rank, in Roman terms, as a general."

"As the commander of the Eastern army, I can create a new General. If I made Kuuli a General in my army. You would no longer have any power over him, am I right? Also, as a Roman general, he would have more power than most kings."

A massive grin came over her face.

"You are…."

The sentence ended; I was engulfed by her arms. It must have been a good idea as Leon and Beaue decided to join in as well.

I called Kuuli into our tent. He stood to attention, waiting for his sentence.

"You have saved my life on many occasions. But! For what you just did, as a member of our tribe, I have to sentence you to death." Began Sky.

He looked stunned, but accepted her judgement.

"Kuuli, you have served Rome on many occasions during this expedition. I have a vacancy for a general, can you suggest anyone who has earned this promotion?"

145

He stood motionless, looking very confused.

"Leave him alone, just tell him his options." I had to laugh; Sky could not keep a straight face for long.

"You have three options. The first is, as a member of the Alemanni, you will be executed. Second option, you can accept my offer to become a Roman general and as such, Sky cannot sentence you. Option three, start running now."

I could not resist adding the third option. Kuuli hesitated, then smiling, he pretended to run for the exit. He then turned and saluted me. "Good morning, commander."

I responded with a salute.

"And a good morning to you, general."

I called all the other generals together and explained the promotion of Kuuli. I was so pleased. He had impressed them with his courage and leadership skills.

"General Kuuli, prepare twenty thousand of the light cavalry. I want them ready to ride in thirty minutes." He saluted again and left the tent.

Sky started to collect her weapons together. I put my hand out to stop her.

"Darling, you are expecting our baby, I can't let you go with us."

She was not happy about that but, in the end, had to accept my decision.

Leon and Beaue, on the other hand, were more than welcome to join us. I had a wagon prepared for the Special team. Now they could travel with us anywhere.

In thirty minutes exactly, we were galloping off in pursuit of Deana and her warriors. She had a half a day lead over us. When we eventually arrived, it was another heart-breaking sight. Thousands of bodies were lying everywhere. These were men who I had fought beside in many battles. I sent Leon and his team to search for any survivors. Every time one of his team found someone still alive, they let out a howl, at which point my soldiers would respond.

Out of two thousand warriors, we only found one hundred still alive, most of them were badly injured. A few had been lucky and were only slightly hurt. From these I was able to find the truth behind this slaughter.

It turned out that Deana, filled with emotion, had led her warriors into a trap. Which proved for many to be fatal.

General Kuuli asked me what I intended to do. I informed him that I had no intention of falling into a trap, as Deana had done. I intended to meet up with King Frome and find out the true situation, before I made a decision.

"Kuuli, if I attack the Lakhmids with my full force, they will Kill Deana and any other survivors, before we can reach them. I am sending you and four of my best fighters to try to rescue them, before I send in the full force of the Eastern army. I can do no more." He thanked me then asked me who would be accompanying him. I turned and shouted.

"Forward!" Then returned to face Kuuli, speaking at a normal volume again. "Here they are. Saxa is their leader, then we have Agi and Auda, followed by Roza. He can steal the last leg of deer from under your eyes. Kuuli was a bit shocked, whilst he saw the advantage of using dogs, he hadn't yet learnt the full advantages of Leon's team yet.

Kuuli and the advance party from the Special team moved off, along the track made by the Lakhmid soldiers. I had my soldiers treat Deana's injured soldiers, then load them into wagons. We then headed south, to meet up with King Frome. I did promise to return his daughter safe from harm. I was not sure how I would explain this little episode.

Kuuli was a good tracker, and Leon's pups were second to none (ok, maybe just Leon) at using their noses. They followed the trail of the Lakhmids for an hour or so, when they came upon a very large encampment. There must have been about nine or ten thousand enemy soldiers. Kuuli had thought about going into the camp and trying to locate Deana. But had second thoughts, as there were so many Lakhmid soldiers. Finally, he decided that when it was dark, and most of the camp were asleep, he would send Saxa and his team into the camp to look for her.

Lucky for Kuuli and his team, the night sky was hidden with clouds. All four dogs sped off in different directions.

The camp was silent, none of the sentries expected any visitors. Saxa and his team were able to move around the camp without detection. Eventually, it was Roza who stumbled upon a tent with ten guards surrounding it. Maybe there were ten guards but most of them were almost asleep. He was able to creep into the tent. In the corner was Deana. She was gagged and tied up. He sped across to her and bit through the ropes that held her. Deana sent Roza back to Kuuli. She felt that she would need support to disable all the guards. Normally she would remove the guards with ease, but that would make noise and she did not think having ten thousand soldiers appearing would help her escape bid.

It wasn't long before Kuuli and all four dogs appeared. The guards were all fully 'asleep' in no time. They were all outside the camp and making their way back to Deana's father, just before the sun began to rise.

By the time the whole of the Eastern army had arrived at King Frome's town, it was almost dark. I therefore decided to leave to attack on the Lakhmids until the morning.

When I had explained how Deana had been captured, King Frome wasn't angry at all.

"I told you that my daughter was headstrong, that is exactly what I would expect her to do." He said, rolling his eyes. I then had a meal with him. Eventually, the discussion regarding Kuuli had to come up.

"Beat, when I let my daughter go with you, to attack the Sassanids, I did not think you would be travelling halfway around the world. And who exactly is this Kuuli?" I was about to speak when he continued. "My daughter is going to marry a member of a royal family. This is how we do things - we make alliances in order to protect each other."

My ears pricked up; he had just crossed a line. Rome had given him more protection that any other local chieftain had or ever could. When we were last here, we paid a visit to the Egyptians to help him out.

"Also, when I have passed on." The king continued. "Deana will be queen of this tribe."

I was now standing up in front of him, his guards drew their swords and Leon and the rest of the team moved between them and me.

"First of all, when I went to Sky's father to ask to marry her, I had only just been promoted to general. A few months beforehand I was a lowly shepherd boy. Of course, her father wanted her to marry royalty, but he accepted me. Why? Because we loved each other. I expect he would want her to reign after he had departed this world too. Sky will be Queen, but I will be the king. Whatever happens, we will rule her tribe and protect them." I was now standing eye to eye with Deana's father. "Kuuli, is a Roman general. These ranks are more powerful than most royals. You talk about alliances with other local tribes for protection, when Rome has given you the best protection possible. At this moment General Kuuli, is somewhere near a Lakhmid camp, containing at least ten thousand soldiers. Why? To rescue the woman, he loves. I am also sure that Deana and Kuuli, whatever they decide, would ensure the safety of this tribe. I am now going to bed, as I have a battle to win on behalf of your people tomorrow. Good night!"

I then stormed out of the tent, followed by Leon and the team, leaving the King speechless.

I rose early, as I had still to make a plan for the upcoming battle. Sky was with me, she may be pregnant, but she still had a very good tactical brain. Also included in the meeting was Marcus, Mae, Lia, and I also asked Datu to attend.

"There are two options," I began. "The first: I surround the town, then fire thousands of arrows, followed by an attack with all the Eastern army. The fault with this plan is that lots of men would likely die on both sides. The second plan is that we fire thousands of arrows, plus throw some of Mae's black bombs."

"Would I be happy slaughtering so many soldiers, my love". Sky interjected. She knew I would not.

Then Datu spoke.

"I know that I am just a villager, but if we approached the camp of the Lakhmids during the night, we could be waiting for them to wake up in the morning."

I considered this plan to be excellent. The rest of the day, we prepared. I also avoided the king.

As soon as the sun started to set, I led one hundred thousand of my soldiers towards the camp of the Lakhmids. I had excluded any of the Ghassanid soldiers. I did this on purpose, for two reasons. The first was to show the King that, once again, Rome was fighting for them. The second reason was that the Lakhmids had attacked soldiers who had been fighting under my banner.

We rode hard all day, and arrived about two miles from the Lakhmid camp about 4am. On our way, we met Deana, Kuuli and the members of my Special team. Deana asked if she could join my attack force. I refused her again.

"Beat, why do you keep refusing my requests to fight against the Lakhmids?"

I had sent five hundred men to their camp, with the instructions of removing the sentries. Of course, the Special team went with them. I kept Leon with me, and I had left Beaue back with Sky. I would not let Deana join us, simply because she would not behave rationally. How could I explain this to her, without hurting her?

"Deana, I am aware more than most people, what a great fighter you are. Many times, we have fought side to side against incredible odds. But, when we are young, we have to learn many things. One of the hardest skills that we all have to learn is how we control our emotions. Do you remember when we passed through the Nafud desert?" She nodded. "Do you remember when I was about to slaughter all the members of the Nabatu tribe, because I was infuriated by the slaughter of the Christian members of their Tribe?"

She nodded again.

"Yes, you even scared me a little as you unleashed your anger."

"Do you remember that Lia managed to stop me ordering the slaughter of thousands, including the old, sick and children?"

My point was now sinking in. She nodded and stood back.

"I will see you when you return, commander".

I smiled, she had understood the message, without me having to mention the massacre she had caused.

I did, however, allow General Kuuli to join us. I believe promoting him was a very good move. For everyone.

When the Lakhmid soldiers rose from their beds, they found that they were surrounded by one hundred thousand Roman soldiers, with arrows aimed at them.

They immediately dropped whatever weapons they were carrying. The ten thousand prisoners were tied up. I then ordered two of my soldiers to go and get Deana.

The ten leading officers were brought before me. I found a chair to sit on. The officers were made to kneel on the ground in front of me. I told Kuuli to find two other seats. This he did, and then he sat on one.

Deana did not take long to arrive. I asked her to sit on the remaining seat. I turned to Deana

"There are the culprits who were responsible for the slaughter of your soldiers."

Deana stood up and looked around the square. Finally, she sat back down again.

"I remember some time ago, Beat. You said that it's not the soldiers who are responsible for killings. It is the officers who give out the orders."

I clapped.

"Well, at least someone listens to me! The question is, what shall we do with these men? I am asking you the question as eventually you will be the ruler of your tribe."

Deana took a while pondering over this.

"Would you like Kuuli to discuss this with you?"

Deana scratched her cheek.

"Yes, Kuuli may be able to help me." The two of them sat away from the prisoners and talked for a good thirty minutes, before Deana finally had an answer.

"As you said before, soldiers have no choice, they have to carry out the orders of their leaders. Therefore, no retribution should be carried out against the soldiers. These," She gestured towards the leaders. "Their leaders, ordered the slaughter of my soldiers and they should be put to death according to the laws of my tribe."

"What is the law of her tribe in reference to this?" I asked, turning to Kuuli. He first looked at Deana before making his reply.

"Death by crucifixion".

I turned and looked at the Lakhmid officers. There was panic in their eyes. Then the officer in command took charge.

"These ten leaders will all be taken with us and presented before King Frome. The remaining soldiers are free to leave."

Two days later we all arrived at the town of King Frome. First, Deana and myself greeted the King. I reminded him about the attack on his soldiers and suggested that I bring the officers in first. The King agreed. The ten officers, with their hands tied, were dragged into the hall. King Frome asked me what I would prefer to do.

"King Frome, my friend, the only way is through a lasting peace. My army will not be here forever to protect you and your people. I personally suggest that you arrange a meeting with the intention of brokering an agreement with the Lakhmids. You have the officers who ordered great suffering on your people to do with as you will. I would also be at the meeting as commander of the Eastern army."

The king smiled and agreed. As the prisoners were being led out of the hall, he then turned to me.

"Now, Beat, what about my daughter and this Kuuli?"

We both sat on our stools.

"Well, as I understand it, you want Deana to marry into royalty. Someone with money and power. Kuuli is now a general in my army. I think you would agree that this surpasses any royalty you could find. As he would be under my direct command, I would decide where and what he would be doing. I was also given treasures by the emperor of the Sassanids. Part of this treasure belongs to Kuuli. If Deana and Kuuli were to marry, I could post him to special assignments in this town. Sky's father wanted the same as you want for Deana, but he accepted me, a shepherd boy. Why? Because we were both in love. And I see the love that Deana and Kuuli share. As the saying goes, my friend, the ball is in your court."

Deana and Kuuli, were invited into the hall next. Deana was beckoned forward first. "My Daughter, you are aware of what I expect from you. To marry someone who is rich and powerful. Also, to be Queen of our tribe when I have gone from this world."

There was silence for a while.

"What do you have to say, Deana?" Deana had been in deep thought, she wanted to obey her father, but she was deeply in love with Kuuli.

"You seem to be having difficulty in talking, my child, let me speak with your Kuuli instead." He approached him. "Young man, is it true that you are a general in the Eastern army?"

Kuuli nodded.

"Yes, sir."

"That you are expecting a share of some treasure?"

Kuuli looked at me, I nodded.

"Yes," he replied.

"If Deana became Queen, would you become her King?"

Again, he looked at me, again I nodded.

"Yes," he replied, nodding firmly.

The king called his daughter forward again.

"Deana, what do you want to do?"

"Father, I love you but I love Kuuli more. He is the beat of my heart."

King Frome sighed.

"Come here you two. Let's get this sorted. I think your Kuuli will make a nice son in law, don't you think?"

They both agreed. I left them having a family chat. I wanted to get back to my darling wife and my brother Leon. We have been together for all of his life. He was fluffy when he was born, he doesn't have that much fur now, but I still call him 'fluff' or 'fluffy'. Not sure what I will call Sky. I guess it's just best to just call her Sky or darling, I don't want to get beaten up haha.

CHAPTER SEVENTEEN

THE HOLY CITY

As I had planned to begin our journey back to Jerusalem as soon as possible, I requested that the meeting with the Lakhmids take place soon. I thought that having my presence there would ensure a peaceful conclusion.

I received the good news later in the day that the meeting had been arranged for noon tomorrow. With this good news I returned to my tent. Sky was silent, which is unusual for her. In fact, even Leon and Beaue were ignoring me.

"Ok, what's up?" They all responded to my question by staring blankly in my direction. "Why am I being ignored?"

Sky turned to Leon and rubbed his head.

"Leon, did someone speak?"

To this, both Leon and Beaue rubbed themselves against Sky. She continued this for a moment longer, then took pity on me.

"My love, I know you have an army to lead… but, don't forget us!"

She was right, I never learnt to delegate properly. Of course, when I was looking after my father's sheep, I always delegated the job to Leon. He would always do a better job than I could have. But when it came to leading the army, I always felt the need to oversee everything.

"Alright you three, I have got the message."

The following morning, I had a meeting with my generals. I explained that I would be delegating more often. I informed the Generals who I would be using the most: Marcus, Anthony, Julius, Flavian and Servius. I ordered Anthony and Julius to prepare the army ready for our return journey to Jerusalem. I planned to leave early tomorrow. I would normally give Marcus more responsibilities, but he would be preparing for his wedding to Lia. Then I returned to my tent.

"Sky, my love, would you like to get together with a few of your lady friends, then meet up with Lia to help plan her and Marcus's wedding?"

I hadn't seen that woman of mine move quite so fast! I wondered what happened to us spending more time together.

Sky did not take much time to get her team together. Apart from Sky and Lia, there was Mae, Deana, Diwa, and Acilla. If I was looking for a fighting force, I could do a lot worse than choosing them. Two other ladies joined them, Beaue and her daughter Frida. I am not sure they could offer much in suggestions, but I could guarantee they would all be safe.

While the women were planning for the wedding, I was able to spend some precious time with Leon. We laid together in the grass, rolling around as if we were still the youngsters - that we were. Then we had a chat. I wanted Leon to train his team to excellence. With special training to Saxa. Then the two of us fell asleep. I can never resist using Leon's head as a pillow.

I was woken up just before noon by General Anthony.

"Time for the meeting Sir."

King Frome was very forgiving. He had nearly two thousand of his soldiers slaughtered, but in order for peace between his tribe and the Lakhmids to happen, he let the subject drop. Both kings needed peace. I stood up and promised the support of Rome, if the alliance came under attack.

"How will Rome protect them, when their armies are so far away?" asked the King of the Lakhmids.

My response settled the peace agreement. I informed both the kings that I was a very close friend of the emperor and empress of the Sassanid Empire. I could always ask them to provide protection if needed. Peace agreed, I needed to prepare for our journey back to the Holy City.

Sky informed me that the preparations for the wedding were going well. Deana had provided some Egyptian cloth to make the wedding dress. Mae and Sky were both going to be maids of honour. Acilla and Diwa were bridesmaids. Datu was in charge of the service in the church. Aris, Axil and Adam were pageboys - I was not sure that any of them wanted this role, but their mum had suggested it.

Leon and Beaue had got their pups ready. They had to use three wagons to hold them all now. I still had two wagons filled with the treasure that Quintin had given me. The last wagon was for Sky to ride in. She was getting big now, no way could she ride a horse anymore.

Early the following morning, we all started back to Jerusalem. Just before we left, I sent scouts ahead to ensure our journey will be easy going. I rode alongside the wagon where sky was resting.

As I rode, I noticed Acilla and Aris seemed to be getting close. I could hear their conversation as I rode. Aris did most of the talking.

"I hear you are the daughter of a general?"

Acilla did not rush to reply.

"Yes, I have a general for a father. I don't know what people have been telling you, but if you want to know more, then ask me."

Aris was a bit shocked by the intensity of her reply.

"Acilla, I am sorry if I have upset you. If you want to tell me more about your father, then I will listen, otherwise let's just change the subject."

She looked at him then started to speak.

"My father wanted to take the army back to Rome. We had completed the emperors' orders. Owing to a promise the commander made to your mother, we had to travel through India, China, and cross the South China seas, which my father did not agree with. We are still trying to return home. My Father made a big mistake in his attempt to return to Rome. He was eventually ordered by the commander to return to Rome with only four other Generals, the ones who had helped him in a ploy to take over command of the army. On their own, I believe they would all have been killed well before reaching Italy. However, Commander Zug informed me that he sent soldiers to follow the generals, to protect them. Since that day, I still have had no news regarding my father."

"Do you think that the Commander should have returned and left my mother all alone in Ctesiphon, with no chance of returning to us?" She was quiet for a while before replying.

"Your mother, through her skills, saved a lot of Roman lives. She even saved the commander's life. Yes, I believe it was right to help her return to her family." There was silence for a moment. "I still wonder if my father is alive."

Aris looked her in the eyes.

"Are you alone now?"

Concern was etched on his face

"I am lucky. Lia has adopted me. She is kind and loving. Although I still hope to see my father again one day."

Aris then put an arm around her shoulders to comfort her. This was the time for me to disappear, I was sure my face had turned red. I jumped into the back of the wagon with Sky.

"How are the two of you?" I asked.

"Don't worry about us," she replied. "Do *you* need to see a physician? Your face is very red."

I had no option but to tell her about the conversation I had just overheard.

"Well, that should teach you not to listen to other people's conversations. Then she grabbed my arm. So, Lia's adopted daughter, and Mae's son are getting close. I wonder if they know."

"Sky, what I heard was a mistake. It's our secret. Let's just leave it at that."

She smiled and patted her tummy.

Although a lot of the scenery was quite nice, it still became rather boring after a while. I decided to pop into the wagon where Leon was. As I expected, he was asleep. Remember he likes three things - eating, fighting and sleeping. I crept into the wagon, then jumped on him. I was lucky that Beaue came to my rescue. I had stupidly forgotten - if someone wakes Leon while he is deep asleep, he will always react as if he is being attacked. Beaue saw what was happening and stopped Leon from causing me any harm. It wasn't Leon's fault; it was my fault for forgetting. We were soon rolling about as if nothing had happened. He was as bored as me.

"Would you like a ride?" I asked him.

He responded by rushing to the back of the wagon. I remembered when, years ago, Sky, Leon and myself were escaping from the Goths. I had attached a blanket made of hide across two horses. Leon remembered this and was soon in the hammock. No Sky this time, the two of us were finally on our own. We were of course riding ahead of the army. After an hour, I got Leon off the horses. We were only a couple of hours' ride away from the coast; we could almost feel the sea breeze.

We both ran about in the meadow, before dropping to the ground. I was laying on my back, looking up at the blue sky, it was so peaceful, I began to doze off a little. The next thing I noticed was the point of a sword resting gently on my neck. If he had wanted to kill me, I would have been dead by now.

"Roman! What are you and that mutt doing here?" I weighed up my options, they were not good.

"If I can get up, I will tell you." I stood up to see Leon tied up and laying on the grass. "We are on our way to the Holy City and we needed a rest."

There were maybe thirty men, who looked like pirates, standing around us.

"Well, Roman, we don't care how you got here, we just want some fun. I have heard about this Roman officer and his giant dog, what was its name?"

"Leon is his name. We will fight your thirty men, and kill them. Just give me my sword." The man talking to me appeared to be their captain. "I am sorry but I will be using your sword. When you are ready, just start, there are no rules". I untied Leon, "Well once again, my friend, we are in a bit of a mess, but we have been in worse situations. Are you ready?"

We stood together, back-to-back, ready for their first attack. Then there was a loud howl, and there was Saxa with four of his siblings. It turned out that he had seen us riding off. He was also bored and raised four of his siblings and they then followed us. As they were slower than the horses they had only just arrived, although just in time. It was now seven against thirty. Then to my surprise there was Roza with my sword. I had to laugh; he could retrieve anything from anyone. I could see where he got my sword, the captain was lying face down in the sand. The pirates attacked; fools, they should have been running away. In a very quick time, the pirates had lost fifteen of their men. It looked like the Special team were also bored.

"Wait!" I shouted. "I can hear horses."

It was my scouts returning from the mission I gave them. At the sight of my scouts the pirates all started to run. Now this is a tip from me - never run from a dog. Why? Because they will pursue you and you won't escape. Leaving Saxa and the rest of the Special team to mop up the situation. I went over to my scouts to get their report.

It turned out that Jerusalem was surrounded by Arabs. I asked them to give me an approximate number of Arabs. They believed there were about forty thousand of them. How could that be? I had left fifty thousand soldiers there!

We all rested on the ground until the main force arrived. When everyone had arrived, I met up with Marcus and Anthony, and Kuuli - he was after all a general now.

I decided to take all my cavalry with me and advance on Jerusalem. The Infantry will stay back and defend the Wagons. This wasn't a fight where I could use my special team, so they stayed behind in the wagons.

On arrival at Jerusalem, I ordered my cavalry to surround the Arab warriors. This was interesting. Inside the walls there should be fifty thousand soldiers. Then outside the walls were about forty thousand Arabs, who were now surrounded by one hundred and fifty thousand of my cavalry. I could of course order an attack and wipe out the Arab warriors. Or the archers inside the walls and the archers with me could all fire their arrows until the Arabs were all dead. My problem was that when I left, I planned to take most of the soldiers, which I left here in Jerusalem, with me. Which would leave Jerusalem open to attack by the Arabs again. I must think of a solution. As I sat on my horse struggling for the answer. Hundreds of horses came into view. I had no knowledge if these were more Arab warriors, or friendly soldiers.

When the dust started to clear, I could see Emperor Quintin at the front of his soldiers. What a relief. On the arrival of the Sassanid soldiers, the Arabs halted. They had been under the impression that they had come to support them.

As Quintin approached my cavalry, he stopped, then waved towards me. I smiled and returned his wave. My horse trotted down the slope to where he was standing.

"You are a welcome sight my friend,"

Quintin smiled.

"It looks to me that I arrived just in time to prevent future problems."

Quintin had messengers sent to the leader of the Arabs, asking him to join us for a talk. The subject was:

'Why do we all want to rule Jerusalem?'

For centuries, either the Christian armies or the Muslim armies ruled this city. In fact, going back further through history, the Babylonians ruled, and the original rulers were the Jewish people. So much blood had been spilt on these walls.

At the meeting, Empress Shirin spoke first.

"All the nations that want to rule this city have a purpose. Jerusalem has holy sites for many religions. The only way to have peace is for all religions to be able to worship in the city."

Her husband then spoke to back up what she had said.

"I am half Roman and now half Sassanid. I understand why Christians want to rule this city, and why Muslims also do. As Jerusalem is part of the Roman Empire, then Rome must be the ruler. However, to keep the peace, I suggest that people of all faiths should be allowed to worship here. I know that this city is at the end of the Roman Empire and to station a lot of troops here could be a problem. I therefore suggest that Rome leaves five thousand soldiers here, and we shall also leave five thousand of our soldiers here. As long as all faiths have freedom to worship, there should not be any problems in the future.

I agreed, and the Arab leader also agreed. I then turned to the general I had left in charge.

"Where are my fifty thousand soldiers?"

"Well sir," he replied. "A large group of Arabs turned up, so I sent forty thousand soldiers after them. Ten thousand are still here in Jerusalem."

I was now too tired to continue this conversation.

"General, I believe you made a mistake sending the soldiers in pursuit of the Arabs, it was clearly a ploy to reduce the number of soldiers guarding the city. Write a report, and give it to me tomorrow." I then gave the order for my army to enter the city and unload the wagons.

I opened the flap to the wagon where Sky was resting. There she was my little angel - she was asleep. We were nearly involved in a battle, but she slept through it. I smiled as I sat on the floor of the wagon. I was about to fall asleep when Lia popped her head into the wagon.

"So... What day will the wedding be?" She said excitedly.

"The day after tomorrow," was my reply.

"What church will we be married in?"

I was knackered, I did not need these questions right now.

"The Church of the Holy Sepulchre. I understand it was built on the spot where Jesus was crucified. I understand that it was built by our emperor." I closed my eyes. "Now please let me sleep."

The following day, Lia and Marcus invited Sky and myself to join them on a tour of the Sepulchre. As churches go, it was beautiful, but I had seen better in Rome. Of course, if this church was built on the Place where Jesus was crucified, what a place for a Christian to be married. I left Lia in the tender care of Sky, who had called everyone over for the final preparations for the wedding. That night passed quickly; Sky was awake most of the night.

Weddings don't do anything for me. I think they are more of a woman's thing. But after the wedding, a banquet was arranged. This is more of an interest for me. I could even see the Special team being fed lumps of meat.

Sky was only about a month away from the birth of our first child. It was an exciting time for me, although I was not sure Sky felt quite the same. It was early summer, carrying our baby in the warmth of the day must have been a challenge. I was feeling very concerned for her having to ride in the bumpy wagon.

I let them celebrate until midnight, when I gave them instructions to be ready to travel at noon tomorrow.

As Sky and myself were returning to the rooms that Quintin had prepared for us. We could hear two of Sky's ladies arguing. They were the ones which Sky had left to look after the pups. We couldn't hear what they were arguing about, so Sky shouted over to them.

"What is the problem?"

The women looked surprised to see us.

"Nothing madame," one replied.

Now Sky knew that there was a problem, so she called them both over.

"Now tell me. What exactly is the problem?"

The two women stood for a while in silence, until they finally decided to open up.

"Madame, we have had great fun looking after Leon's pups. The situation, however, has now changed a bit, in fact it has changed quite a lot..."

It was now the turn of the other maid to join in.

"Leon's pups are now full-grown adult dogs. With all the urges that come with the hormones." Sky was now standing with her hands on her hips.

"What are you trying to say? Come on, tell us."

The maids looked at each other again, then the first maid began to speak again. "Please, would you both follow us?"

We both followed them, we were heading towards where the Special team were housed. We entered the house and climbed the stairs. We did not have a clue as to what we were going to see. Eventually it was all revealed. The door to what seemed to be a very large room opened. Sky and I looked at each other before bursting out laughing. The sight revealed to us was a room full of puppies of various ages. There had to be at least twenty. We turned to the maids, who were standing behind us. Sky spoke first.

"Is there something you would like to tell us?"

Now it was the second maid who spoke first.

"Well, as we were saying, Leon's pups are grown up now, and they are full of hormones. Do you remember sir, when you were in your teens?"

I stopped her there. I was well aware of my hormones, and was fully aware of what she was trying to tell us.

"So, these are Leon and Beaue's Grandchildren?" I could not stop laughing. "Leon is a granddad! Let's see, do you know Sky, Leon is eleven now."

Sky laughed.

"And you are nearly thirty!"

I responded to this statement sharply as I think most people would. I didn't like thinking about turning into the next decade.

"I am twenty-nine, not thirty! Anyway, you are twenty-eight."

It was time to stop.

"So, you have hidden these pups?" I said, turning back to the maids.

Looking embarrassed, the first maid replied.

"Sorry, it's nature."

I slapped both of them on their backs.

"It's ok, I will now have a larger Special team. And We will find more hands to support you. Is that, ok?"

Their problems had been listened to and help was on the way, they were very happy.

I immediately ordered ten of my soldiers to support the maids with the fast-growing pups.

Then I grabbed Leon and Beaue. Follow me Leon, or should I say *granddad*. He was aware of all the pups, so I told him to organise something. At this moment I was not sure what.

That was the first good sleep I had had in ages. We both got up together - I don't know why Sky got up, she has little to do until the baby is born.

Marcus was organising the army, ready for our departure. I took Anthony aside.

"Anthony, please come and help me. I would like you to organise all those pups, get them integrated as part of the team. He saluted and promised to do his best.

Just one thing to do before leaving - I had to say farewell to Quintin and Shirin. It was a sad farewell. I did not like Quintin at first, but I eventually grew to like and respect him a lot.

Eventually the long hall started. As we left the city, there was a huge line of people that seemed to go on forever.

I turned and waved farewell to everyone.

CHAPTER EIGHTEEN

URGENT MESSAGE FROM ROME

We departed at noon, when the sun was at its highest. My idea was that in a few hours, the sun would start to set, and the weather would get cooler. My priority was Sky. She was due anytime during the next few weeks. I found I was riding my horse less and less, instead spending most of my time in the wagon with Sky. There seemed to be an endless line of friends visiting. The first was Mae, -as Mae had three children, she was the one with all the experience. Lia and Deana, often called round. The continuous stream of visitors continued. I decided to sit up front. Here I could feel the breeze as the wagon slowly headed west. An amazing sight came into view. On the right-hand side of my wagon, was a mass of dogs, from adults to puppies. It was Leon and Beaue, taking their extended family for a walk. I jumped out of the wagon and ran over to Leon.

I grabbed him and tried to pull him over for a wrestle. We had done this thousands of times. On this occasion I had a shock, Leon held his ground, and I went flying over him. Leon had a stern look on his face. He then returned to walking his family. I got up and stood rubbing my chin, it looked like Leon was training his family at last. I followed them for about a mile. For many years we have been like brothers. Now he had a family, and I would become a father soon. This was the first time I had seen him as a trainer. Every now and then they would all stop. He would divide the pack into smaller groups. Second in command was young Saxa; he and Leon worked together. Although Leon and Saxa thought they were totally in command of the pack, I could see two others who no one would challenge - Beaue and her daughter Frida. I was pleased that I would now have a large and fully trained Special team. It was time for me to hop back into the wagon, my walking days were far away now.

There were still lots of visitors filling the wagon, so I thought I would pay a visit to Lia, and see how the education for Adam and Axil was getting on.

I jumped on my horse and rode over to where Lia and Marcus were. When two people are just married, they seem to be floating on a cloud. It was a wonderful time in one's life. Lia confirmed that their lessons were going well, and that she thought that both Adam and Axil were very bright lads.

Marcus then asked to speak with me. We both rode ahead of Lia's horse. He reminded me about the incident on our way past Sidon.

"Remember," he said, "before we left, you had all the soldiers' thumbs cut off. It's possible that there could be trouble on our return."

I had to admit, I had forgotten about that.

"You are right Marcus, there may be some reprisals as we pass Sidon. They would avoid a straight attack, but they could cause some minor problems. Take Anthony and Kuuli, also ask Datu to go with you. I need to know if there could be any problems before we get close to Sidon."

Eventually I called a halt. It had been a long day, and we all needed a rest. I had been riding in the wagon with Sky for most of it. I asked her if she would like to go for a walk. She was more than up for that. I helped her out of the wagon, then we walked over to watch Leon and the Special team in training.

If I had known what was going to happen, I wouldn't have gone. Sky had stopped to stroke one of the younger pups, I say younger, but she was about a year old and an Antolian Shepherd Dog is almost full grown at that age. I continued walking towards Leon. He had been talking to his team about something, then to my complete shock, he rushed towards me. Then he jumped and knocked me onto the ground, before clamping his jaws around my throat. For a moment, I thought that he had gone mad. He then jumped off me and turned to his team again. I was still recovering from the shock, when I turned over on my side, watching what Leon's attack on me had to do with training. As I watched, an unfortunate soldier was passing by. I saw Saxa creeping towards him. Then it happened. Yes, he had the unfortunate soldier on the ground with his jaws around his throat. When Saxa had returned to the pack, I helped the soldier up.

"Sorry, they are in training. Please inform my generals that the men should be aware that they could be involved in the Special team training, as you just were, if they pass this way."

The poor man had not fully recovered as he staggered away. Sky had been watching. She was still laughing when I caught up with her.

"If you keep laughing like that, you will give birth here."

I took her back to the wagon, then went over to where Mae and her family were camped. I asked how everyone was, then I asked her extended family if they would like to do some sword practice. They were all bored of travelling, and jumped at the chance of some action.

Mae was of course always ready for some swordplay. Datu had little knowledge of fighting with a sword, but he was strong with good reflexes. Then came the older, well I can't call them kids, as seventeen is classified as adult. Aris, Diwa and Acilla were all becoming more than useful with the sword. Also, at the age of twelve and thirteen, both Axil and Adam were improving well, however they were both excellent with the bow. They all took turns practising with each other. I wanted to spend more time with Datu. I knew he was strong with quick reflexes, and he had made his own sword (well, he was a blacksmith).

I was correct, he was strong, but easy to sidestep. His defence was good, and with his reflexes he often blocked my strikes. After a while, I told Datu to stand back and watch. I then asked Mae to spar with me. She jumped at the chance to fight the commander of the Eastern army.

When it comes to fighting with the Sword, Sky was probably the best in my whole army. Mae and I were almost equal. At martial arts, few are better than little ol' Mae. But with the bow, I had practised for years in the mountains guarding my father's sheep. Few were better than me. My strokes were more powerful than Mae, but she was quicker. Sometimes she would also throw in martial art moves. If you were not ready for these, you could suddenly find her behind you. After an hour's practice, I asked

Mae to teach her husband how to fight with the sword. I then took the remaining five towards a small corpse of trees. I selected a few targets, then arranged a competition. They were all becoming excellent archers, but Axis and Adam were a step above.

Time flew by and it was soon time to eat. I returned to the wagon, expecting a nice meal. It's ok, I don't expect Sky to cook - I have a maid who prepare the meals.

I opened the flap at the back of the wagon. I was greeted by screams of "Get out and close the flap!"

Sky's water had broken and our first baby was on the way.

I took a deep breath and climbed into the wagon. I immediately got into an argument with one of the women who was helping to deliver our baby. I told her that I was going to support my wife during the birth of our child. This woman shouted at me.

"Men cannot be present!"

I was about to throw this woman out of the wagon when Sky spoke.

"Let him in, he can hold my hand during the birth."

I was happy, I had won this round. I held Sky's hand, and whispered words of encouragement. I have no knowledge at all about childbirth, simply because men are not allowed at the birth of their children. I was about to learn something which will live with me forever.

First came the pain. Now Sky is a very strong woman, but she was screaming in agony. I was holding her hand and as the excruciating pain increased so did the strength of her grip on my hand. Her nails were digging into my skin - it felt like I was being tortured. But it was nothing compared to the pain my beloved sky was going through. Tears started to form in my eyes. As her husband I felt helpless, the love of my life was suffering and there was nothing I could do to help her. If all husbands watched their wives suffer like this, I don't think any babies would be born.

Then an amazing sight occurred, our baby's head popped out. Then out came the rest of it. The lady who I had been arguing with held our baby and smacked its bottom. There came that wonderful sound of our baby's cry. She was going to show the baby to Sky when the other lady told her to wait as Sky wasn't done. She was pushing again. Another head popped out; Sky had produced twins. What a girl, no wonder she was so big! The first was a boy, and we also now had a daughter.

Sky was laying in the makeshift bed with our babies in each arm. I wish I had an artist with us, it would be so good to look at a painting of that scene in the future. Then a truly special moment. My babies were passed to me. I held them in my arms and looked into their eyes. They say that the eyes are a window into your soul. I indeed felt that I was looking into their souls. I turned to Sky and looked down at her.

"I am so proud of you, my love."

We both started to cry tears of joy. Eventually I left Sky to rest, and the maids looked after our babies. As I left the wagon, I was thinking about how my dad would love to see our babies.

I had to break the news to my brother, yes Leon. I rushed over to where the special team was still in training. I called Leon and Beaue over.

"I have a surprise for you both... I am now a daddy!" Wow it felt good to say that.

I opened the flap which served as a door to the wagon.

"Sky," I called "You have two visitors." At that point two heads poked through the flap. Followed by two furry bodies.

Leon wanted to lick the babies but he was stopped by Beaue. It was a time for looking, not licking.

While Leon and Beaue inspected our babies, we discussed their names.

"Darling, shall we give them tribal names?" Sky thought for a bit then replied.

"How about choosing their names from the Bible?" I liked the idea.

"Can we name our son after that David who was a shepherd, then became king?" Sky agreed, then offered a name for our daughter.

"Can we name our daughter after Deborah? She was a prophet, judge, a military leader, plus a songwriter and minstrel. Her people gave her great love and respect. Her name means 'bee', as in a honeybee."

"So, we have David and Deborah, great names my love. I am sure they will both grow up to be great leaders."

I had just experienced the most memorable time of my life. Sky had been in so much pain, but when her babies were born, she seemed to have forgotten everything that had happened beforehand. Watching her looking down and smiling at her twins, gave me a warm feeling in my heart. I crept out of the wagon - they all had a hard time and were now sleeping. I stood outside the wagon, in silence, feeling lost on an island somewhere.

My mood soon changed when I was approached by Datu. He gave me their report, after scouting the area surrounding Sidon.

When we passed Sidon on our way to Jerusalem the first time, the city was in the hands of the Sassanids. Since then, we had agreed to a peace treaty with the emperor. I now had two problems. The first was: do the Sassanids in the city know this? And, if they decided to vacate the city, would I have to leave some of my soldiers to garrison the city? I decided to take twenty thousand of my heavy cavalry with me, and pay a visit to the city.

On arrival, I was invited into the city for a meeting. Dream on! I would need to be stupid to get myself trapped inside the city with most of my soldiers outside. In the end they agreed to meet outside. I was correct, so far, the news of our peace treaty had not got to them. They informed me that they could not leave until they received orders from the emperor. I had no choice but to accept his decision. The good news was that they agreed to stay inside the walls of the city until my army had passed. After receiving this good news, we returned to the rest of my troops.

One thing which kept worrying me, was the fact that I had all their soldiers' thumbs cut off the last time we were here. Would they just leave this be and move on? Or plan some form of revenge?

I couldn't get back to our main group fast enough. I climbed into the wagon, expecting to see Sky still in bed. I had forgotten, lying in bed is not my Sky. The maids told me that they were looking after the twins. Sky had left the wagon half an hour ago. I rushed to the exit and jumped out. This wife of mine, who had given birth not that long ago, was now practising her sword fighting skills with Deana. What am I going to do with her?

I called a meeting with my generals. I informed them about my meeting with the Sassanid commander. I also told them that we would ride past the city of Sidon as if we were friends, although I did share my concern about reprisals. I suggested that we keep the wagons in the middle, the infantry would ride either side and the heavy cavalry would be at the front and back. Finally, the light cavalry would ride on both outer sides, giving us a fast response to any problems. To me, it was a good plan. However, this would leave the Special team, who ride in a few of the wagons, taken out of any action, as they would be stuck in the middle.

Two miles from Sidon, I called a halt. We needed to consider what preparations would be required. In order to be prepared for any negative moves by the Sassanids. Twenty-four hours would be enough time.

The next stop would be Antioch, then home. We could then show our babies to our fathers. They would be so happy to see them. We had been away for nearly five years! I did miss my father. I often thought about the times that I roamed about freely in the mountains with Leon. Our lives have changed so much since then. We are both fathers now, with all the responsibilities that came with the role.

"Commander! We can't find Mae or Diwa. Please help us commander."

It was Mae's family; they normally call me Beat - I presume they were now calling me commander because they were so worried.

"When did you last see them?" I asked. "They both said that they were going to collect berries."

Datu looked very worried. What to do? I could get two hundred thousand men to search for them. But I had a better idea.

"Call Leon and the Special team!"

Leon and his team were with me in no time. They were led to the spot where Mae and Diwa had last been seen. It did not take long before the team got the scent. Leon looked at me. We were so close that we each knew what the other was thinking. He was telling me that this was a job for his team alone. As the Special team took off to find the girls (Mae would like me calling her a girl), some of my soldiers started to follow them. I ordered them all to stay here. This job was for the Special team.

Mae and Diwa had gone looking for berries. One of the maids had told her that she had seen some bushes near the stream. True, the berries were there, ripe and juicy, but the problem was that a group of Sassanid soldiers were hiding behind the bushes. They were both taken by surprise, and were quickly tied up.

The Sassanids knew they could not attack us in force, but they could try to sabotage us. In this case they had captured two of our women. They planned to offer them back in exchange for something that they had not decided on yet. Then their leader came up with what he believed to be a brilliant idea. He sent a message to me, saying that if I want to have the woman back in one piece, they wanted half our food, and I had to have my thumbs removed. The other option was to watch Mae and her daughter be slowly killed. I nearly forgot. No Reprisals!

Leon and the Special team lost no time in catching up with Mae and the Sassanids. There were maybe thirty soldiers sitting around a fire and the two women were both tied to small trees. Leon and Saxa chatted about what action they should take. There were in fact thirty-two soldiers, where the Special team only consisted of twenty-seven, which included many pups. The pups were maybe a year old but this was their first proper fight. They decided that the five youngest would have the job of releasing the woman. The rest of the team were outnumbered but surprise was a great equaliser.

Leon and Beaue took half the team, while Saxa and Frida took the rest. It was late, only the animals of the night could be heard. Twenty-seven more animals joined them. Silently they approached the camp. They waited while the young ones took the two guards out. Then just as efficiently freed the women. It was now time for the rest of the team to go to work.

They crept into each tent, then worked their way around the tents, putting the soldiers out of action. The whole action was over in less than half an hour. The women tied all the soldiers up, then, somehow, they managed to lay the soldiers over their saddles. Agi was the strongest in the team, and also the fastest. He was sent back to me. His instructions were to get me to bring soldiers, to help bring the enemy soldiers back. Leon is multi-talented, but even he couldn't pick up a soldier and throw him over his saddle. Mae and Diwa performed an amazing task. They were almost back at our camp, when we finally met up with them. I praised the team to no end. Mae and Diwa also amazed me. They showed no fear, and kept strong throughout.

When we were about four hundred yards from the walls of Sidon. I had all the prisoners brought out. They were thrown on the ground.

"Can you explain why these unfortunate souls kidnapped two of my women?"

After a short wait, someone replied.

"They have nothing to do with us. Kill them."

I informed them that I believed him to be a liar. I was then thinking of actually attacking the city. Lucky for all concerned, to our surprise, Emperor Quintin arrived just in time. He explained the current events to their commander. Then he withdrew all his men and women from the city. As he rode away, Quintin looked at me and smiled.

"It's all yours now Beat. Then after giving a wave, he was on his way back home."

We all camped outside the walls overnight. I finally agreed to leave five thousand men to protect the city.

That's five thousand in Jerusalem, and five thousand here. Lucky for us the next stop was Antioch. Then just a boat ride, a short walk and home.

"Sky, I can't believe it. After five-year travelling, we will finally be home!"

I took advantage of our last night there. I picked up Leon, and the two of us went for a walk. First, we stopped to chat with Lia and Marcus.

"I presume you will both be settling in one of your villas, Lia?" She smiled and told me I was correct. "I am leaving Julius and Flavian in command of the Eastern army when we leave. Marcus, you can have a month with your wife before your duty will call you again."

Next, we went to see Kuuli and Deana.

"What will your plans be in Italy? I expect General Kuuli will get some time off."

Deana smiled.

"Lia has given us some of her land as well as Mae, we will be ok."

We completed our walk, by dropping in on Mae and family. They were all happy, with a new start in life. One thing was certain, they have all deserved every happiness.

Leon returned to his family, while I went back to my wagon. There was Sky, looking as though she had never been pregnant. I am so blessed that she loves me.

The following morning, we started the final section of our five-year tour of the East. The navy should be at Antioch waiting to take us back to Ravenna. Once we embarked, we would be only half a day from Rome. 'I think I will spend the whole day relaxing with Sky and the twins', I thought. Of course, Leon and Beaue would be with us. Just lounging by a pool, drinking wine - I mean Sky and I of course, Leon and Beaue would have water.

When we eventually arrived in Antioch, I took Sky and the twins to a hill overlooking the sea. It was a beautiful day. The sky was a dark blue, and the sun seemed to skim across the waves.

"Darling, it's been a long journey, but we will be home soon." We later returned to our room. I then decided to visit Julius and Flavian and clarify the change of command. As I was returning to Rome with Marcus. Julius and Flavian would be in command of the Eastern army until new orders arrived. General Kuuli would also be going to Rome with us. It had been a long journey, but it was all over now.

Or so I thought. Sitting across the road, I saw three men in officers' uniforms drinking wine. This aroused my curiosity. If they were part of my army, they would not be sitting there. If they were not in my army, then who were they? I walked across to where they were sitting with Marcus. I stood in front of them and took a moment to realise who they were.

"Well, I never! I was wondering what happened to my generals. I am truly glad that you are alive."

The men looked up and stared at me.

"Marcus please get Acilla and bring her here."

Yes, it was three of the generals I had sent back to Rome. I was happy that they were alive, Acilla would be so happy to see her father. I informed the three generals that I had forgiven them, and that they should return to their legions. All was wonderful, until a rider came galloping into town. As soon as he was near me, he jumped off his horse. Then saluted.

"Sir! I have a Message from Rome."

I took the message and started to read it.

ROME HAS BEEN SACKED BY THE HUNS

THE HUNS ARE RAVAGING ITALY
THE COMMANDER OF THE NORTHERN ARMY
HAS NAMED HIMSELF AS EMPEROR OF ROME

YOUR ORDERS:

- FREE ROME
- DRIVE THE HUNS OUT OF ITALY
- MARCH TO BRITANNIA AND TAKE
THE USERPER PRISONER

Lightning Source UK Ltd.
Milton Keynes UK
UKHW011829260522
403577UK00001B/75

9 781665 598880